Torment and Tarnish

Adventures of a Villain-Leaning Humanoid

Book Two

Jamie Jackson

CONTENT/TRIGGER WARNINGS

Psychic/mental coercion, blood & gore, sex & sexual acts, harsh language, animal death

CONTENTS

ACKNOWLEDGMENTS

Thank you, once again to my husband and children, for always being there

Thank you to Jennifer, who continues to suffer through reading my first drafts

CHAPTER ONE

If you don't remember me from last time, I'm Megaera, Meg for short. Just to recap for you, a power stealing murdering demon creature made me his next target. Some hero took offense to that and tried to rescue me, which didn't go well for him, and I got stuck picking up the slack. Apparently, the result of that is I have a new name: Vengeance.

No, I did not learn a lesson from my brush with death.

I'm still petty as all get out.

And I still don't do drugs.

Oh, and the hero and I? Ended up being a thing. Shut up.

Let's get started.

∞

"Try it again, Meg!" Virgil, known as Vigilante to heroes and the public, was calling to me from the roof of his compound. He was up on top of the hulking stone structure because it was the one place he could be well out of range of the perimeter of the fear compulsion while being able to view the full circle of it. He had taken up his thinking position, one arm crossed over his chest, one hand up at his chin, fingers resting against his dark beard. He had left his duster inside the compound, and his t-shirt was clinging to his wiry frame. It was one of the few times I had seen him without his jacket, and his sleeve tattoos stood out against his pale skin: abstract lines, bars, and triangles in black.

Right? Who would've thought Virgil's got tats?

I sighed. "It's not going to get any bigger. That's the range."

"Oh, I'm sorry, are you an expert in this?"

"It's my power! I should know!" I shouted back, frustrated. We had been at this all morning. I had barely finished my cup of coffee before he was herding me out the door to see if I could expand the range. After a short break for lunch, we were right back at it.

"Try again anyway."

I gritted my teeth and shoved my long, black curls out of my face. I was so going to unhook all his TV cables when we were done here. He's lucky that's all I was planning on doing. But I called to the whispers again, and they came. The figures curled down around my arms, stretching their way out. Shadows elongating from my feet along the ground. They rustled their way through the grass. Virgil won't mow it, so it stays long and unkempt. He won't trim any of the bushes either. At this point they resemble small trees because of their size. The whole aesthetic of the property is best described as abandoned.

Ten feet in all directions: that's how far the figures and shadows went. So if you want to get technical, a twenty-foot diameter. But for future reference I'm calling it ten. Don't argue the semantics with me. Ten feet away, they stopped and wouldn't go any further. Even though I pushed, they stayed there, swirling in place, a circle of inky black and smoke.

Virgil watched me, arms crossed, head tilted to one side. "I know for a fact you've hit targets from farther."

"Because I had a target!" I snapped. "This is guard mode; they're not going to expand the circle farther than that." Also, at the time, I had been *pissed*.

2

"It's your power. Tell them to."

"Tried that. They listen about as well as I do." Yes, I got stuck with the power that operates on independent thought. Go figure.

That earned me a chuckle from Greg, who had just landed next to Virgil on the roof. He was brushing his blonde hair off his face, doing the "cool dude" movement, the one where the guy uses the whole of his hand, fingers first to push the hair back. Did I take a minute to take in his broad shoulders, the flex of his muscles as he moved? You know I did. A girl's got needs.

You can't tell me you don't check out your, well, whomever you're seeing. Boyfriend. Girlfriend. Nonbinary partner. Whichever. I don't judge.

Moving on, Greg doesn't have tattoos because he can't get them. The needles can't get through his skin to deposit the ink, and the gun would just break anyway. I can, but I won't because, needles.

Virgil just sighed. "Okay, let's take a break. I mean, unless you want to be a target, Greg?"

"No," I said. Greg, however, was silent, watching me seriously. "*No*," I repeated since emphasis seemed required.

"I could—" he started.

"NO," I interrupted him.

"Well, okay. Scrap that one," Virgil said. "I'm not getting into the middle of another lover's spat." Virgil disappeared toward the back of the roof, and I could hear his boots clanging against the metal of the ladder he had used to get up there.

Greg floated down to me. "I would be fine," he said.

"No, Greg," I said. I couldn't do that to him again. I had promised, and I don't care what he thought about being fine. Physically, sure, my power couldn't touch him. But mentally? I didn't want to test it. Also, I wasn't entirely sure that the whispers and figures would attack him at this point. The one time he had gone down, when Red Eye had almost killed him, they had ended up guarding his body, and I hadn't told them to.

I hadn't told either him or Virgil that they had done that on their own.

Greg threw an arm around my shoulder and pulled me into his side. "Okay," he kissed the top of my head.

Virgil had come around the front and pulled the door open. He looked back at us. "Are you coming? Because I'm locking it behind me, and I don't care if you sleep outside."

We followed him in and then went ahead as he spun the lock shut but got stuck waiting at the door down to the main living area. There was no handle, and he had locked that one too on the way out.

"Hey, Virgil, if you die on a mission, how are we supposed to get in?" I asked. I mean, yeah, morbid, but I'm nothing if not practical. Okay, sometimes I'm practical. A little bit. Okay fine, almost never. It was still a reasonable question.

He gave me a startled look. "I – hmm, I've never had to consider that before. I'll have to set up a way for you and Greg to get in and out without me. I'm tired of unlocking the doors every time one of you gets back anyway."

Don't get excited. I haven't done any hero shit. I only left to go get new clothes because some jackass stole my stuff from my apartment while we were off on our previous adventure. Well, I mean, it didn't have a front door, and the landlord decided they didn't need to bother with any sort of impediment to people who didn't belong there. And Greg is still negotiating with his previous employers about retrieving his personal belongings from his apartment. They wanted him to come in and fetch his (and what there was of my) stuff in person, but he thought going in was a bad idea. Just because he could break his way out didn't mean he wanted to waste the time doing it if they thought they could trap him.

They had sounded extremely nervous about him being freelance and not under their purview. He was lucky he had been in the middle of negotiations about renewing his contract when the whole thing with Red Eye went down. Otherwise, things would've turned out a lot worse for both of us. Bending the rules of your contract is one thing, outright desertion another. You don't fuck with the US military.

Either way, yay for renter's insurance! The one time I actually listened like a bona fide adult, so I got my pay out for my stuff being stolen. I mean, I wouldn't have normally because no police report, but I had Fortress backing me up. And I might have marched down to the adjuster's office and scared the daylights out of her when she told me she was going to have to refuse my claim. Shh, Greg doesn't technically know about that one. He thought he took me into town purely so I could cancel my insurance. Also, no, Virgil still won't let either of us drive his cars, or I would've gone by myself. Plus, I don't have a license anyway. What? Some of us can only afford public transportation. Cars require money. And most of mine went to rent and shit. A car wasn't on the table.

Yeah, you heard me right. If Virgil would let me drive his car, I would do it sans license. What? Like you wouldn't. The Cobra is a classic.

Anyway, I don't have a policy anymore. But I have clothes, so there's that.

Also, no, I don't have a paycheck yet. Virgil is negotiating with his "patrons" for adding us to his team. I hear it's going well.

What? Look, if some idiot is going to pay me stupid amounts of money to check their attic for them, fine. What am I going to find? A raccoon?

Once we were downstairs, I tried to go sit down on a couch since I knew Greg and Virgil would head for the kitchen. Greg didn't let go of me. Instead, he steered me away from the seating, practically frog marching me down the hall. "Uh uh," he said, "I could hear the two of you arguing from a mile away. I know what you're going to do." With his super-hearing, for Greg that might not be an exaggeration. I've never asked him what the actual range is.

5

"I wasn't going to do anything."

"It took him an hour last time to fix all his books."

"I wasn't going to touch the books."

"Keep it up and next time you move his stuff around, he's going to stand there and make you fix it yourself."

I smirked. "I'd like to see him try and make me do anything." Virgil at least had a healthy amount of respect for what I could do. Which might be because he had to burn the entire contents of his bedroom the first time he saw the full results.

"You wouldn't," Greg admonished me.

"I wouldn't," I agreed, but only because it was Virgil. He's not that bad once you get to know him. Just don't let him drive you anywhere.

Greg dropped me off at the kitchen island and started pulling things out of the fridge. "Hungry?" he asked me.

"Virgil and I ate while you were gone."

Virgil came in behind us, settling on the stool next to me, close enough that our legs brushed. He does it purely because it aggravates Greg. I could see him clench his jaw. Greg might still be a bit sensitive about other people being near me ever since I got tortured and almost murdered, and then someone he trusted tried to kidnap me out from under his nose.

I looked at Virgil. "Bubble. Stop getting in it."

He cleared his throat and shifted his stool away. "Sorry."

Greg didn't look up from the pepper he was chopping. "BulletProof wanted me to give you a message."

Virgil narrowed his eyes. "What's the message?"

"When are you next going to be in town?"

"That's a question."

"His message is the question."

"Well, the answer is no."

"No?" I said, confused.

"I don't date heroes," Virgil explained.

"Is it because you have terrible taste?" I asked.

6

"No. My taste in men is fine; it's my taste in women that's terrible. I just don't date heroes. I don't want to end up on the wrong side of a lover's spat over the right way to approach things."

"Won't work with other heroes, won't date other heroes—" I said.

"I work with you two."

"Not a hero," I told him.

Virgil pointed at Greg.

"Doesn't count," I said.

"How does he not count?" Virgil argued.

"You two know I'm right here, right?" Greg said.

"Oh, that reminds me. I forgot to give this to you this morning. Salary advance." Virgil pulled a folded check out of his pocket and handed it over. I unfolded it and then choked.

"What the shit?!" The number of zeroes on the check looked like way too many.

Greg leaned over the counter to take a peek. "Where's mine?" he asked.

"Yours got direct deposited because I have your account info."

Greg narrowed his eyes. "When did you get ahold of that information exactly?"

"Wouldn't you like to know?" Virgil said. He tapped the check in my hands. "Make sure you set some of that aside. You'll get a 1099 at the end of the year. You're officially a contract employee."

"I'm going to have to go into town to deposit this," I said. "Mobile deposit won't let me put that much in at once."

"I'll take you after lunch," Greg said.

"Training is after lunch," Virgil said.

"We already had lunch and just did training," I argued.

"After Gregor's lunch," Virgil said. "We still have the rest of it to complete."

Yes, you heard that right. Not only is he being a power range expansion fanatic, Virgil is making me do *physical training.*

Run laps, jump over things, tuck and roll. I don't plan to be getting into any one-on-one melees with villains or anything. Most people with powers also have increased durability. Nothing like what Greg has, but enough. If I try to engage someone in physical combat, on the other hand, I'm going to lose. Really, really badly. So in case we end up with another Red Eye situation, Virgil wanted my ability to run away and live to fight another day to be top notch, and Virgil is nothing if not an exacting taskmaster. It's a stupid argument because outside of Red Eye no one is going to be able to get close enough to me to physically fight me. What's the likelihood we run into someone who can turn superpowers back on heroes a second time?

"It'll take us all of an hour," Greg said.

"Fine. We'll just extend training by an hour to make up for lost time," Virgil said.

I groaned.

"Complain all you want," Virgil said. "But you'll thank me later. We're doing laps when you get back."

Which meant Virgil was going to chase after me in his version of tag. At least the things he was trying to hit me with were relatively soft. Chalk bombs basically. Initially it had been paintballs, but to get them to burst, he'd had to use more force than he expected. He couldn't just lob them at me with his telekinesis; he had ended up having to shoot me with them, and the rather spectacular set of bruises I had gotten from that had caused an argument over his methods.

So, Virgil and I had a discussion, and even though we both agreed Greg was overreacting, we decided it wasn't a hill we were willing to die on.

I'm not kidding when I say Greg is really sensitive when it comes to me right now. He had nightmares for weeks after Red Eye died. I would wake up to him sobbing and calling my name in his sleep. If I thought I fell hard, it made me wonder if Greg had fallen just as hard or if it was related to being a hero and a moment where he had failed at protecting someone he set out to keep safe. But I haven't asked, and he hasn't said. And I haven't told him I know about those nights either. If Red Eye hadn't been very, very dead when I got done with him, I would have worried he was behind Greg's nightmares.

All of that is just to say that Virgil and I were trying to be considerate of his "protect Meg at all costs" needs, but within reason. We were all learning to work well together, and that meant neither Virgil nor Greg hid relevant information from me. And I tried not to go flinging myself into danger any time one or both of them pissed me off.

Which, when no one is trying to murder you, is insanely easy to do. Also, where am I going to go? I don't have a ride without one of them. And I'm not stealing one of Virgil's cars. I'm not that stupid.

I guess I am hiding information, but what I'm keeping to myself is pretty "need to know" stuff. Virgil had already suspected my control over the whispers wasn't complete, but he figured that out on his own, and he totally told Greg. I just haven't mentioned that they view us as belonging to each other, and apparently people I feel safe with also qualify as "ours." Haven't told them that.

I also haven't told them about the dreams I've been having. Of sand, and sea, and an olive grove. Sometimes, when I'm awake, I can hear the waves crashing in my ears and smell the salt in the air. There's a memory there, if only I could remember it. But it won't come.

"Need us to pick up anything while we're in town?" Greg was asking Virgil.

"No. Have you tried checking with Striker about your things?"

"No," Greg said, pulling out his phone and tapping away. "Now I have. Good call because he can just overload the locks." His phone pinged back almost immediately. "Perfect. Meg, you ready?"

"Yup," I said, hopping off the stool.

Virgil followed us out the doors. "Fly safe. Don't hit any

geese."

"That only happened the one time," Greg protested.

"You hit a goose?" I asked.

"Yes, and he's never let me live it down. I regret ever telling him."

"There were feathers stuck in his hair. I would've known even if he hadn't told me." Virgil's lips were twitching.

Greg sighed, scooped me up and took off.

∞

Greg dropped me off in an alley near the bank. Because I made him. What? People don't need to know I've got my own personal flying chauffeur. Plus, I'm still not cool with heights. I need a minute to calm down after every trip.

"You'll be okay?" he asked me, one hand cupping my face.

"I'll be fine. It's the bank. Stop freaking out."

"Hmm," he said, and kissed me before he took off. He was supposed to be meeting with Striker to pick up our stuff while I got this check deposited. Striker had agreed to go around the bosses and retrieve our things for us. I believe his exact quote had been, "Fuck these bitches. Hold me a freelancing spot. I'm up for renewal in twelve months."

Guess the politicians were having trouble in the ranks without the glue that had held them together, which was kind of my fault. Sorry not sorry, Bolt. Greg had put in an appearance at the funeral, not just because it was expected, but because they had been friends, or at least friendly before her sudden but, according to Virgil and his recordings of her conversations with someone unnamed, inevitable betrayal. It would have been odd for Greg not to attend. Fortunately, my presence was not required.

I left the alley passing by a wall mural on the way depicting a peacock, eyes in the feathers where the spots would be. It was impressive; whoever had painted it was way more talented than Mirage. His had been exclusively landscapes. And not particularly well done. They were blobby.

When I got inside, the bank was busy. It was one of the larger, older ones with the marble or stone floors, from when they cared about aesthetics. I joined the line for the tellers, arranged in switchback style marked off with ropes. And waited. And waited some more.

Then someone decided to get into my personal space to my right.

"Yo," he said. "You come here often?"

I turned my head and scoffed. Typical bad boy: biker gear, stubble, dark-haired and eyed. You know the type. Think Pedro Pascal as Oberyn. Look, I gave *Game of Thrones* a try, just this one episode because everyone was freaking out about it. It was too bloody for me. *The Mandalorian* is a better show anyway. It's got Baby Yoda. Oh yeah, Virgil totally got Disney+ just for me. Ahem. Anyway. Moving on.

Biker Boy's eyes were traveling down my body. "My face is up here," I said. "And you can back up now."

He smirked at me.

Oh, okay, buddy. I'm gonna wipe the floor with you in a minute. Just as soon as I get this check deposited and don't need to worry about the tellers being too scared to deal with me. I rolled my eyes and turned my head back to face the front.

He leaned over so that his head was hovering over my shoulder, his voice in my ear. "You're gonna wanna get behind me in a minute."

Behind him for what?

The doors at the front of the bank slammed open, and I, along with everyone else turned to see what the commotion was as several men in ski masks came striding in. They were armed, and they were yelling. "Everyone down!"

People were screaming and throwing themselves to the floor, and Biker Boy grabbed my shoulder and shoved me down. "That's my cue," he said, throwing me a wink. I smacked his hand away.

"Hey, boys!" he yelled, and then he was engaging the closest one, moving fluidly through the air, and he was fast, like a striking snake. The first guy went down like a wet sandbag. One of the others rushed to take a hostage; the rest aimed at Biker Boy.

"Don't move!" they were shouting.

"Or you'll what?" he shouted back, beckoning them. "Come on, try me."

"Oh, for fucks sake," I muttered, as I stood up and called the whispers. This idiot was going to get people killed with his showboating. Me included, and I didn't have time for that shit. The figures were at my back, the shadows reaching along the floor.

The screaming that had subsided into tears and terrified murmurs started again. People were scrambling to get away from me and the sudden unease floating in the air as the whispers sighed. The figures and I moved forward, as they swirled outward ignoring the other patrons. They wouldn't touch them with anything other than the fear, and that we couldn't help.

The eyes behind the ski masks were confused for the moment it took me to get in range, and then they were screaming, too. The fear and fury made them turn on each other and do most of the work for me; even as the figures tore into them, they were ripping at each other. When the last one dropped, I let the whispers go.

The bank was suddenly quiet, the silence broken only by sobs. Biker Boy was staring at me. I turned around and walked up to the teller. Anyone who had been in line ahead of me that hadn't gotten out of the way crawled hurriedly away from me. The whispers were gone, but they had just watched me make people tear themselves apart without raising a finger, so I couldn't blame them.

I set the check on the counter. "Can you deposit this for me?" The teller stared at me white faced. "Well?" I prompted. She looked down at it, back up at me. Nodded. Slipped the check back behind the partition.

"Account?" she croaked. I inserted my debit card into the keypad and entered my pin. Clicking of a keyboard on her side. When she was done, she handed me a receipt. "You can access two hundred dollars of that amount now. The rest can take up to ten business days to be available." Her lower lip was quivering. I felt guilty, because usually I don't have to deal with the aftermath of what my power does to the people I'm not aiming it at. Well, I also generally ignore it, but I really needed to get this check deposited, and now thanks to those idiots with ski masks I can't come back to this specific bank.

"Thanks," I said. "Sorry about the mess." I turned around and headed out the front doors.

Biker Boy followed me. "Hey! Hey!" he yelled. I ignored him. He caught up to me. "I'm talking to you!"

"That's nice. I don't want to talk to you."

He grabbed my shoulder. The whispers howled.

He didn't react. The other people on the sidewalk did, ducking away and running, leaving clear space around us. He locked eyes with me, his hand still on my shoulder. One of the figures swiped at him, ripping open his jacket sleeve. "Shit!" he yelped, yanking his arm away. They had tagged him; I had seen the blood already dripping off his hand. "Who are you?" he demanded.

Greg landed next to me, placing one hand on my back. I could feel his arm trembling as he pushed past the fear around me. I let the whispers go, turning to look up at him. He was staring down Biker Boy. "You might want to go," Greg told him.

"Nice welcome wagon you two have here," Biker Boy said. He held out his unbloodied hand. "I'm Ranger." Greg didn't move, so Ranger dropped his hand. "Well, I'll be seeing you around." He winked at me, before mounting a red and white motorcycle parked at the curb. He revved the engine and took off, sans helmet.

"You okay?" Greg asked.

"I'm fine." But the fear hadn't touched Ranger, and I had never had that happen before.

"We need to tell Virgil."

"Hmm," I said. Guess Greg saw the whole interaction. He scooped me up and took off.

Virgil already had the doors open when we got back. "What happened?" he demanded.

"New guy in town," Greg grunted.

"I know that," Virgil snapped. He was following us in, locking the doors behind us as we headed downstairs. I could hear the news anchor he had up on the TV talking about the attempted bank robbery. They had already managed to get ahold of the security footage.

"Well fuck," I said. The camera hadn't managed to capture the whispers, figures, and shadows, so all you could see was everyone suddenly fleeing away from me before the robbers turned on each other in a frenzy. I'm not even sure regular people would be able to see the figures if they had been captured on film, since they can't see them anyway. The news had a very grainy, blown up image of my face they were putting up in a corner of the screen. They just kept playing that clip over and over again. Ranger was the only person who stood there, just staring at the carnage going on around him. I hadn't noticed at the time. "Fuck," I repeated.

"What happened?" Virgil asked irritably this time.

"Bank robbery?" I said weakly. I was still processing the fact that now *everyone* would know what I could do. This was going to end up being national news. No way was it staying local.

"I can see that," Virgil said. "Who the fuck is that? Why is he just standing there?"

"Um—" I'm nothing if not eloquent in these situations.

"He said his name is Ranger," Greg crossed his arms. "And it would appear he's immune to Meg's power."

Virgil's brow furrowed. "I need to make some calls," he

14

said before he headed down the hallway.

The news anchor was still talking. I could hear the words but couldn't take in the meaning of them.

"Meg," Greg's hands were on my face, his eyes on mine. "It's okay. Breathe."

"I'm on the news."

"Uh huh," he said. "Happens to me all the time. Give them ten minutes; they'll get bored."

"Bored?" I squeaked. "I'm on the news! I don't want to be on the news!"

Greg pulled me into him, my head pressed against his chest. "Meg, breathe." I could hear his heartbeat in my ear. His arms felt warm around me. He had put his nose in my hair again. I took a breath. We stood there until I was done panicking, and then I tried to squirm back. Greg kissed my head and let me go. "You okay now?"

"Yup," I said. "All good. Go do something heroic so they put you up there instead."

He chuckled and pulled me back into him. "I have a better idea to take your mind off it."

"Get a room, you two," Virgil said from the hallway. "Or you can come hear what I found out."

"Again with the timing," Greg grumbled. "What did you find out?"

"Ranger," Virgil announced, reading off his phone. "Fresh from the city of Lorraine. Before that, Garro, and RB. Moves around a lot. He can manipulate time, has hero-standard general hardiness, and has a penchant for predicting when things will happen. Apparently, he couldn't predict you, Meg. My contact says he's already put out feelers asking around about you."

"Great," I said. "So, like, what? We're immune to each other?"

"I think that would require further meetings between the two of you to figure out."

"No thanks," I said. "We done here?"

"Don't you at least want to hear my theory?" Virgil said.

"Not really." The fact that someone was immune to the compulsion the whispers put out had left me feeling unsettled, and I didn't want to continue discussing it.

Greg snorted. Virgil shot him a look. "Well, I'm telling you anyway. I think his immunity to you means you're a wildcard. He can't predict you *because* he's immune to you."

"Exciting," I said. "What's for dinner?"

Virgil spun around and stalked off toward the kitchen. "My genius just goes completely unappreciated."

Greg sighed, "I think you actually managed to hurt his feelings." He looked down at me. "He likes you, Meg. Don't take that for granted."

CHAPTER TWO

I ended up pouting in the living room for a while because I knew Greg was right, and I hate being wrong, which happens a lot of the time. I just didn't used to be too concerned about the effect it had on people.

What? I can be introspective.

I ended up tracking Virgil down before he left to do patrols in the city for the night. He was in the garage tinkering with the engine in his Cobra. He didn't look up when I came in. I watched him for a bit, cooling my heels, and because I can't stand silence, I ended up being the one to speak first.

"What're you doing?"

"It had a misfire the last time I took it out," he grunted.

"Oh," I said, because I had no idea what that meant.

He sighed and straightened up, pulled a rag out of his back pocket, and started wiping grease off his hands. "Did you need something?"

I stared at the floor. "Sorry," I said. I sounded grudging, even to myself, so I cleared my throat and tried again. "I'm sorry I don't appreciate your genius more."

I was surprised when he chuckled. "Apology accepted," he said, and he patted me on the shoulder. I craned my neck down to look at my shirt. He had left a greasy handprint on the white cotton.

Guess I'm not the only one who can be petty. I totally deserved it.

"We even now?" I asked.

"Oh, not even close," Virgil said. "You missed training."

"That wasn't even my fault," I protested.

"Whose fault was it then?"

I was silent, because I was the one who had been rude and then pouted on the couch until I got over my snit. I should've known that Virgil would've put aside any hurt feelings he had if I had come to him sooner. He wasn't easily ruffled, and currently he was patiently waiting for me to answer him.

"Mine," I grumbled.

"Yours," he said. "I would appreciate it if you would take both my time and yours seriously. You're playing with the big boys now, and you need to be prepared. It won't all be bank robberies where you're the only shark in the water."

Suitably chastened, I looked down at the floor. "Okay," I said, and then, because I couldn't help myself, I hummed a few bars.

"What are you singing now?" Virgil asked.

"*Playing with the Big Boys* from *Prince of Egypt.*"

"Kids' movie?"

"Maybe."

"Hmm," he said. I took the chance to retreat before he found a task for me to do.

I could hear him humming the song as I went back up the stairs, and I giggled.

∞

Both Virgil and Greg went out, leaving me alone in the compound, and they still weren't back when I got up the next morning.

I checked my phone while I made coffee. No missed calls, no texts. So I sent the same text to both of them: "?????"

And then I waited.

Nothing. Now I was starting to get nervous, because Greg always answers me, and it's rare that Virgil won't answer.

I tried calling both their phones. Greg's went straight to voicemail. Virgil's rang, then voicemail picked up. I left messages on both.

I turned on the news in case there was anything there.

My face was still front and center.

I waited, hands clenched in my lap through the news cycle. The anchorwoman finally got to a different subject.

"A bridge collapse last night in George Harbor—" and there was Greg, pulling cars out of the water. The news anchor was continuing, "—left 15 dead. Experts say the death toll would have been higher if not for the quick action of Fortress." I let out the breath I had been holding.

Okay, but where was Virgil?

My phone pinged. I looked down at it, a text from Virgil, "Don't watch the news, I'm trying to squash it."

Squash what?

They were back around to my face, and the news anchor had moved on. "In breaking news, KBC has an exclusive interview with the parents of the unknown hero from the attempted bank robbery of yesterday," she smiled at the camera. "Tune in at 6:00 to find out who she is."

The whispers screamed, and the figures lashed into the TV. The screen broke; it sparked and then hit the wall, rocking back from the force of their passage. And then they were gone. I stood there for a moment, staring at the TV before turning for the stairs.

I had to get out. I needed air.

How could they? How could they go to the news about me? Nine years with no contact between us, and the first thing they do when I surface is go to the reporters?!

I went up the stairs, spinning the locks open in a daze.

Greg was at the front door. "Meg, thank God, I've been trying to get your attention for an hour – Meg?"

"Why didn't you just call?" I whispered.

"My phone, I didn't think," he pulled it out. "I went into the river with it still in my pocket. It's full of water. I'm sorry, I didn't mean to—"

"Mean to what? Mean to leave me here not knowing what happened to you?" I was shouting at him. The anger at my parents was boiling up and spilling out on him, and the whispers began clamoring at me to let them out. They would help me find my parents if I asked. I wouldn't ask. I could feel the tears start welling in my eyes.

"Meg, I'm sorry." He reached for me, and I jerked back from him.

"Don't touch me," I spat, part fear, part rage because what if I couldn't keep the whispers back and they hurt him? I could never forgive myself, and I could feel them pressing against my ears.

He looked like I had slapped him. And in that moment, what could I say?

The gate slammed open. Virgil.

Greg cleared his throat. "I'll – I'll see you inside." And he went in.

I sat down on the steps and watched Virgil's car come in. Even after the ramp closed, I didn't move. Eventually the whispers sighed and quieted. I stayed on the steps, sniffling and angrily wiping the tears away. The door behind me stayed open.

This is another one of those things I haven't told Greg or Virgil. They know I'm not on speaking terms with my parents, but I haven't told them why. I'm sure they have their theories, but they've never asked me about it. I would find a way not to answer them anyway.

Eventually I heard footsteps. They stopped behind me, and Virgil sighed. "You watched the news, didn't you?"

"Yes," I said because it seemed pretty obvious. There was no way he missed the condition the TV was in.

He sat down on the stairs next to me. "Was I too late, or did you just ignore my advice?"

"Too late. But I wouldn't have listened to you anyway," I admitted.

"You never watch the news."

"You were both still gone when I got up."

"Ah," said Virgil wisely. "Greg is distressed."

I studied my shoes.

"Checking to see if they're in your mouth?" Virgil asked dryly.

I laughed. And then sniffed. Scrubbed at my cheeks. "I'm sorry."

"I'm not the one you should be apologizing to this time."

Silence.

"I know," I said. "I just…" and I sighed. Because I just what? Just kept screwing up? Lashing out at people who were on my side? Both honestly. And I couldn't explain why. This moment with my parents and the news - it wasn't like this was the first time I had reacted like this. The whispers responded to me, to my emotions. I couldn't just blame them when I acted like an ass. And what would I tell Virgil that he didn't already know?

"I have some advice," Virgil said. "Don't push him away. Because if you do it enough, eventually he won't come back."

"He's still friends with you," I said.

"He's not in love with me," Virgil said. I could feel my heart stutter, turned my head, a half-formed protest on my lips, but Virgil was still speaking. "That affords me a level of detachment where he can let things roll off his shoulders. Don't look at me like that. He's not the only one who can read what's not said."

I cleared my throat, looking at the hands twisted in my lap. "He hasn't mentioned anything like that to me."

Virgil shrugged. "He will when he's ready. If you don't drive him off before that point. Now, I have people I have to go yell at to try and make them retract that exclusive story announcement they just shared."

But was I ready to hear it?

I sighed and followed him inside.

Greg was standing at the bookshelves flipping through a book. It was upside down. He looked up and shoved it back into a random spot when he saw me.

"Hi," I said.

"Hi," he said.

"Hello to you, too," Virgil said dryly.

Greg's lips twitched. I was fighting not to smile. Virgil gave a long-suffering sigh and pushed me toward Greg. He met me halfway, wrapping his arms around me.

I took a breath, burying my face in his chest. "I'm sorry."

"Hmm, could you repeat that? I couldn't hear you," he said.

I snorted. He absolutely heard me. I pulled my head back. "I'm sorry."

He put a hand on my face. "I'm sorry, too. I didn't mean to worry you."

"I broke Virgil's TV."

"I saw that. He's going to make you pay for it."

"Still right here," Virgil said.

∞

Virgil found us still in the living room seated on one of the couches once he got done with his calls.

"Fucking reporters," he snarled. He flung himself into the chair across from us. I tensed.

"They're still going to run the story?" Greg asked.

"I've gotten them to take it back to the editing floor so they're not using Meg's real name. And they're supposed to be blurring your parents faces and modulating their voices while they're at it. But yes, they're still going to run it. Just not today."

"How'd you accomplish that much?" Greg asked.

"I went to the head of the studio and told him I know exactly how much insider trading he's been doing."

Greg shoved his hair back. "Jesus, Virgil."

"Friends in high places," Virgil said. "I don't want him in jail; he's not useful that way. He put pressure on his reporter because his reporter told me she's not scared of me."

"Did you tell her I'm the one she should be scared of?" I asked.

Virgil chuckled. "No. Because you're not a villain."

"Eh," I said, with a so-so motion of my hand. "It's a fine line."

"It is," Virgil agreed. "Oh, one other thing, she wants to come along on a patrol."

"No," Greg said.

"Not with you. She wants to go with Meg."

"I don't do patrols," I said. "I don't do missions. I don't do hero." Training and admonishing from Virgil aside, I'm most definitely still not a hero.

"Your paycheck says otherwise."

Damn it. Guess I'm going on my first patrol.

Virgil was continuing. "She wants us down at the docks. Something illegal coming in. So, we stop the shipment and send her off on patrol with Meg to see what else turns up."

"Is it drugs? It's drugs, isn't it?" Greg said. "It's always drugs."

Virgil shrugged. "It could be."

Greg sighed. "That used to be below my paygrade."

∞

Is it a requirement that docks be creepy at night? I mean, like seriously creepy? Because they are. The fog, the slap of water on concrete, the way sounds are muffled and directionless.

Virgil drove us in his Hummer. He used to correct me

that it's a Humvee, as in the real grade A military vehicle, but gave up and now he's just calling it a Hummer too. He wanted something heavily armored in case it wasn't drugs. All three of us had discussed the possibility that someone was inevitably going to try to shoot at me. Even though Virgil had given me an outfit lined with Kevlar throughout most of it (I mean, I still needed to be able to move, the joints aren't covered, and Kevlar is kind of thick), we also needed to worry about not getting this reporter killed, so we had come to a decision she probably wasn't going to like.

She was waiting for us when we came in, leaning against her car, arms crossed. As we were unloading from the Hummer, she came striding up to us. Typical bulldog reporter, reasonably dressed in clothes she could move in, but still had that smooth, professional feel because she had to be ready for the camera. Her blonde and highlighted hair was pulled back into a sleek ponytail.

Which made me very aware of my curls, hanging heavy against my neck and shoulders.

"I was beginning to think you weren't coming," she said, coming up on Virgil's side. "What's the plan? Where do you need me? I can stay back a bit, but I need to be able to see."

Virgil chuckled. "Oh, no. You're not coming in with us."

I could see her eyes narrow as I came around the car, and then her face cleared. "This her?" She held out a hand to me. "I'm Susan." I didn't move. She slowly dropped her hand.

"Play nice," Greg murmured in my ear as he went around me.

"Fortress," Susan smiled. "Always nice to see you. Good work on the bridge."

"Susan," Greg grunted.

"So, you were saying? About me not coming in? Because I feel like I am."

"You," Virgil said, "are going on patrol with Vengeance here so we don't have to worry about you getting shot."

"I'm wearing Kevlar—" Susan started to argue.

"Your point being? Your intel was incredibly light on details. We don't know what we're dealing with. Fortress and I don't need the distraction."

I could see Susan opening her mouth to protest.

"Ah, ah, ah," Virgil said. "I can call your boss again."

She shut her mouth and scowled at him. "Fine," she said and turned to me. "Are we going? Do you mind if I record? I'd like to interview you while we're patrolling."

The whispers were there, sighing in my ears. Figures curling around my legs, shadows pooled at my feet. "If you can stand being that close to me."

"Hmm, I'm made of pretty hardy stuff," she said. But I could hear the tinge of unease in her voice.

"Vengeance," Greg huffed, I could hear the laughter in his voice.

I let the whispers go. "You and names," I teased. He chuckled, came back to me in a stride. His hands hovered for a moment, but he didn't touch me.

"You'll be okay?" There was concern in his eyes.

"You always this protective over heroes you send out?" Susan asked, interest sharpening her tone.

I could see Greg's jaw tighten; his lips were pressed in a thin line. I realized, even though he couldn't help but ask me if I could handle it, he was trying not to give her any fodder, and for that I was grateful. But screw her if I'm going to let fear of what she would say run my interactions with him. So I rose up on my toes, one hand on his neck and kissed him. He responded, one hand in my hair, the other on my back as he pulled me into him.

I could hear Susan fumbling for something.

"That's off the record," Virgil said firmly.

"But—"

"Off the fucking record," I could hear the warning in his voice.

Greg pulled back, one hand on my face. "Watch

yourself," he said seriously.

"They've got to watch out for me," I said and smiled at him. He chuckled, kissed me again, and then he and Virgil headed past the gate and deeper into the docks, leaving me alone with the reporter.

"So," she said, "how long have you and Fortress been a thing?"

"I don't know what you're talking about," I said, turning to face her.

She narrowed her eyes at me. "Vigilante's been giving you pointers, hasn't he?"

"No idea what you're talking about," I said cheerfully. I started off up the street, away from the entrance to the docks themselves. She scrambled after me. We were walking past warehouses, no streetlights, just the exterior security lights for the buildings, so we were mostly surrounded by the night. Right now we were on the main strip, the area between each building creating its own alley, a maze of metal siding to our sides.

"How long have you been working with Vigilante?" she asked me. She had pulled out a handheld recorder and was speaking into it before holding it out toward me.

"I haven't kept track."

"How about how long have the three of you been working together? Fortress didn't used to team up with him."

I shrugged. "Haven't kept track of that either." I mean, I honestly hadn't. The whole Red Eye thing and the aftermath had felt like something of a blur. It had been long enough that Greg's nightmares had stopped and I was healed up from when Red Eye had gotten a hold of me, although I had been left with thin lines of faint scars white against the dark olive tan of my skin, my knee still pops occasionally, and my collarbone aches any time it rains.

"According to your parents you demonstrated this ability early on—"

I turned on her, the whispers pressing against my ears.

She took a hurried step back from me. "I don't give a shit what my parents said. You are going to stop talking."

"Why?" she asked. "Did I hit a nerve? Is your relationship with your parents contentious?"

"I don't know what you're talking about," I snapped. "But what I do know is if there is anything going on around here that I need to handle they can hear you from a mile away. Which means they'll be gone before I reach them. So shut up."

She stared at me hard for a moment. Then she clicked off the recorder and put it up. "Fine. But I want a real interview with you after this."

I snorted. "Good luck with that." I continued down the street, the whispers curling along with me. She left some space between us as she followed me. I could hear her frustrated mutters, so I stopped and turned to face her again. "Do you have a problem?" I asked.

"Why can't I get close to you?" she hissed at me.

"I don't know, maybe you need to grow a spine?"

"My spine is fine," she said, irritated. "What are you doing?"

"Walking," I said. "But if that's too much for you, maybe you should just go home?" The whispers giggled.

"You," she said accusingly, "are doing something that means I can't get near you." She was sweating, and there was a tremor in her voice, but she wasn't backing any further away.

The figures brushed against my shoulders. "Whatever you say, but I'm—"

There was a scream. I snapped my head around to face the sound.

Silence.

Then another scream.

"Stay here," I ordered, and then I took off. The figures swept ahead of me, searching. I went racing down an alley, shadows sliding down the walls with me. Two alley cats scrambled out of my way. I stopped. Again, silence. The whispers and figures swirled around me. Was the scream I heard just the cats?

Footsteps. The heavy tread of boots.

I withdrew into a doorway, the metal cold against my fingers where they were pressed against the door, the figures curling with me.

The footsteps went past me. They walked right past me as if they couldn't feel the aura of fear surrounding me.

I stayed still against the door.

The footsteps stopped, the vague figure they belonged to only a few feet away from where I stood, crammed into the doorway. The whispers were curious. The fleeting tug of a memory, but we waved it away; we didn't have time for remembering.

The figure turned.

Nope, fuck this. My experience with Red Eye meant I wasn't taking any chances when my power wasn't working right. I shot out of the doorway and sped down the alley away from whoever it was.

There was a startled exclamation. Footsteps chased after me. "Stop!" a voice yelled.

I skidded around a corner, bounced off a wall and kept going. Cries went up around me as the figures and I swept by a group of people who had been huddled against the alley walls.

I cut around another corner. Dead end. Fuck.

I backed up into one of the corners, crouching in the darkness, the figures brushing my arms, shadows reaching out along the ground from where I planted my feet.

My heart was hammering in my chest. If I screamed, could Greg hear me at this distance? I wouldn't entirely mind the assist.

My follower came up the alley and paused by the dead end I was hiding in.

Why does this shit always have to happen in the dark? I'm going to tell Virgil I'm only taking day shift from now on. Look, just because this is my first patrol doesn't mean I haven't heard the horror stories from other heroes.

Okay, fine, just the stories from Greg and Virgil. I don't talk to any other heroes.

The figure chuckled. "There you are." He started toward me.

I darted out of my corner, and what felt like a gust of air blew over me. I didn't stop, I just dodged around him.

"What the fuck!" he said.

But apparently the surprise didn't last long because he grabbed my arm, swung me around and then slammed into me, pinning me against the wall before I could get clear of him. "You!" he said, and I could hear the recognition in his voice. At this distance, even in the dark, I knew exactly who had been chasing me. I could see his face.

The figures slammed back, long fingered hands slashing up his sides. He screamed and stumbled back from me. They withdrew, swirling and curling around me, shadows rearing up darker than the night around us.

"Don't touch me," I snarled.

"Whoa, okay, okay," Ranger said, hands up, palms out. "How'd you do that?"

"Do what?" I sneered. Because it was a stupid question. How do any of us do what we can do?

"You didn't stop." He sounded confused.

"No shit," I said. "Why would I?"

"You—" and now his tone was aggravated, "Who are you?"

"I don't have time for this," I said impatiently and went to step around him. He moved in front of me, and another gust of wind swirled around us. The figures billowed out so that he was forced to back away from me or get sliced again.

"How are you doing that?" he demanded.

"You sure repeat yourself a lot," I snarked. "Now if you'll excuse me, some of us have places to be." I moved to leave, but he stepped in front of me again. "Move," I growled. The shadows swirled and he stumbled back.

"Okay, okay, just quit with the freaky shit. I just want to

talk to you."

"And I don't want to talk to you," I said sharply, moving around him. He finally stopped trying to block me, but he still followed me. The shadows formed a wall between us.

"Would you stop? I'm not going to hurt you."

"Keep following me, and *I'll* hurt *you*," I said.

Racing footsteps came down the alley, and then Susan was there, panting and out of breath, just feet from us, where she had stopped out of range of the whispers, figures and shadows surrounding me.

"Vengeance, there you are. Jesus, how long were you planning on leaving me there?"

"Until I got back," I said. Ranger chuckled and I shot him a glare. "I'm not here for your entertainment," I snapped at him.

"Who's your friend?" Susan asked me, all business now that she had gotten her breath back.

"We're not friends," I said at the same time that he said "Ranger."

Susan held out her hand. "Nice to meet you, I'm Susan Rodriguez. Reporter for KBC."

He shook her hand and looked over at me. "Interviewing for the news are you, *Vengeance*?" I didn't like the way he made my name linger in the air.

"She's trying not to," Susan said, all smiles at Ranger. "How long have you two known each other?"

"We don't know each—" I was saying but Ranger interrupted me.

"Oh, what, two, three days?" he smirked at me. He turned back to Susan. "I'm new in town. I would love to talk to you, have someone show me the sights. Vengeance says she doesn't have time." He shot me a wink.

"Great," I said. "You two have fun. Bye now." He gave me a startled look. Ha! Take that jackass, I'm not rising to your bait. I headed down the alley, and now Ranger was trapped being polite with Susan, who was pelting him with questions as she pulled out her recorder.

Guess he overestimated my desire to investigate mysterious circumstances and men.

CHAPTER THREE

Greg and Virgil were already back at the Hummer by the time I got there. Greg was pacing, Virgil leaning against the car.

"She's fine, she can handle herself," Virgil was saying when Greg spun in my direction. The relief on his face was palpable as he rushed to me and swept me up.

"Um, hello," I said. "Not that I mind the enthusiasm, but what's up?"

"Where's Susan?" he growled, setting me down and stepping back, but he kept his hands on my waist.

I waved vaguely. "Back there with Ranger somewhere. Why?"

"Her intel was bad," Virgil said. "What do you mean back there with Ranger?"

"I mean he was wandering around the alleys, and I left the two of them being all chummy. Her intel was bad how?" From the way Greg was holding onto me, something more was going on.

"It wasn't a shipment coming in," Virgil said.

"And?" I prompted.

"Well, whoever it was on that ship, they did a lot of damage on the way out. And they were long gone by the time we got here," Greg said.

Well, that explained why Greg was pacing by the car

instead of out searching for me. The danger was technically past, and he was giving me time to deal with anything that had cropped up.

Didn't mean he dealt well with waiting though.

"Let's go," Virgil said. "Before Gregor has a heart attack from stress."

∞

We were lying in bed, Greg drawing circles on my back before he finally got around to what was bothering him.

Of course, he can never just start with it. "Meg," he said.

"Hmm?" I said sleepily. I won't tell him, but I like the way he says my name. Although, he probably knows.

"I think I liked it better when we weren't asking you to be a hero."

I turned my head to smirk at him. "I tried to tell you I'm not a hero," I teased.

He sighed. "I'm serious, Meg. We're asking you to do things that are dangerous, and all I can think about is how vulnerable you are."

I propped myself up on my elbows, lifting my head to look him in the eyes. Dark and worried, his eyes looked back at mine. "I'm less vulnerable than I was," I pointed out, because it was true. I had barely been tapping the full potential of my power when we met. Besides, I hadn't exactly been a soft target then either.

He put a hand on my face. "But you could still get hurt. Anyone who can get past the fear, anyone who figures out where it's coming from - they can go after you. You don't have the higher resistance to damage most of us have."

"I know," I said. "It's totally unfair."

He smiled, but the worry wasn't gone from his eyes. "The last time you got hurt, you didn't wake up for four weeks. Virgil couldn't tell me what was wrong. He didn't know if it was a symptom of something Red Eye had done to you or something to do with your power. I didn't know if you were ever going to come back to me." He had both his hands on my face now, his fingers tangled in my curls, a hitch in his breath.

"I can't lose you," he said. "Meg, I—" I kissed him, because I still didn't know if I was ready to hear what he had to say. Because he would want an answer, and I wasn't ready to tell him. He would know what it was in the beat of my heart.

He would be happy. But he would want to make plans for the future, and I wasn't ready for that either. And then he would know that too. I've never been good at the important conversations.

So instead, I made sure he forgot he had something he meant to tell me in words. Because that way, if it had to, my heartbeat could lie.

∞

There were waves crashing against the shore, rushing water coming up over my feet, swirling against my ankles and then retreating. I could feel the wet sand under my soles, the pull of it as the water dragged it away, washing it back out to sea.

The smell of salt in the air, the wind tugging at my hair. The curls brushing against my neck where it had come loose from its coiffed style.

Megaera, said a voice, sighing on the wind. A messenger.

I could ignore the first message. In fact, he would expect it. I had always been capricious.

Remember, said the whispers.

But remember what?

∞

There was an insistent buzzing coming from the security room when I walked by it on my way to the kitchen the next morning. I ignored it because I was heading for the coffee pot, and I found both Virgil and Greg in the kitchen, also ignoring it. I stopped in the doorway. They stared at me.

"Are we all ignoring that?" I asked.

"Yes," Virgil said, taking a sip of coffee.

I headed for the stools at the island because Greg had put down his mug and was pouring coffee into another one for me. He slid it across to me. "Why?" I asked. "I mean, I know why I'm ignoring it. Why are you two ignoring it?"

"It's Ranger," Greg grunted, and he looked particularly put out.

"How long has he been out there?"

"Hmm," Virgil checked the time on his phone, "about an hour now?"

I watched them both, thinking. "How'd he get your address?"

Virgil set his cup in the sink. "That I'm not sure of. Someone would have had to give it to him, because I have this thing hidden under so many shell companies it's a forensic accountant's worst nightmare."

The buzzing continued.

"I don't think he's giving up," Greg said.

Virgil sighed, and headed to the security room. We followed him. He hit the button for the intercom, triggering the crackle of static. "Fuck off," he said and hung up. We watched Ranger on the screen. He hit the callbox. Buzzed it again. When that didn't elicit a response, he started to head for the gate itself. "Fucking idiot," Virgil muttered. But he hit the button for the intercom again. "I wouldn't do that if I were you." Ranger raced for the box, but Virgil had already hung up. Ranger hit the buzzer again. He was looking around, then yelling at the cameras mounted above him.

I snorted. Greg leaned against the doorway. "Should we try talking to him?" he asked.

Virgil sighed, and hit the intercom. "What do you want?"

Ranger stood there, silent.

"Look, you've got my attention, but my patience is short so either you answer, or I hang up again."

"Oh, so you're actually talking to me now?" Ranger asked.

"Okay, bye no—"

"Wait, wait! I want to talk to Vengeance."

Virgil looked over at me, muted the intercom. "He wants to talk to you."

I shook my head.

"She doesn't want to talk to you," Virgil told him.

"So, she is there?"

Damn it.

Virgil chose to answer his question with a question of his own. "Who gave you my location?"

We watched him cross his arms. "That's for me to know."

"Well, then I can't get Vengeance to talk to you," and Virgil hung up.

"I'm not talking to him," I said.

"Just wait," Virgil said.

Ranger buzzed the callbox again. Virgil smiled. "Now what do you want?" Somehow, he kept his tone modulated to one of irritation.

"BulletProof told me where to find you. He said if I talked to you, you would know where she is."

"Thanks so much," Virgil said, and hung up again. "And that is why I won't date heroes. Bunch of gossips. Present company excluded."

Both of them looked at me. "What?" I asked.

"You didn't say you're not a hero," Virgil said suspiciously.

"Hmm," I said, taking a sip of coffee. "Whole thing might be growing on me."

Ranger was out there most of the day. At first, we were just going to wait for him to leave, but as the day wore on, and he continued to hang out there, occasionally trading where he was sitting from his bike to the ground, to a log lying by the road, Greg was starting to get impatient, and the constant on and off buzzing of the callbox was wearing on his already short temper. It was wearing on all our tempers. Virgil had even declared the day training-free because if we went outside, Ranger would be able to hear us.

Eventually Virgil decided to take pity on Greg, probably so he wouldn't end up breaking something irreplaceable. "Why don't you two take off? It's not like he can follow you in the air."

"I don't know that we should be taking Meg on patrols when there's an unknown out there."

"Not patrols," Virgil said. "I meant *out* out. Take a break, get dinner. Go incognito. No one can ever pick us out of a crowd without a costume on anyway."

I snorted. "You guys stick out like sore thumbs. There is no such thing as incognito."

"I'm sorry?" Virgil said.

"I can spot a hero out of costume from fifty feet," I told him. Although Ranger hadn't given me that vibe at the bank, come to think of it. He should've though; he definitely had the strut. Maybe I was just too miffed at the obvious eye fuck he was giving me to notice at the time.

"Well, incognito or not, why don't you two dress up, go somewhere nice and I'll keep our guest distracted."

"I know a place," Greg said.

"I don't have anything dressy," I said.

"Shopping first."

"You're gonna take me shopping?" The last time I had gone to get clothes, Greg had dropped me off and disappeared.

"Yup, I'll hold your purse and everything."

∞

Greg cleans up pretty nice in a suit. I didn't even know

37

he owned a suit.

He took me to a little boutique store, where I ended up with a little black dress and heels that I'm positive cost more than the rest of my wardrobe. He and the salesclerk were in on it to keep me from getting a look at the price tag. But I'm pretty sure she works on commission, so I don't blame her for following his lead. Especially since he's the one in the suit whipping out a credit card, and I'm over here in torn jeans and a tee.

What? Those jeans are my favorite pair. Do you have any idea how long it takes to break those things in to optimum softness?

Also, now that I think about it, the whole situation was a little *Pretty Woman*-esque. If he teases me with a necklace in a jewelry box, I'm out.

The restaurant that we ended up at was when I realized I was way out of my comfort zone. No prices on the menu, and everything was in French.

It was small, intimate, and intensely romantic. The kind of romantic where the only tables are little two seaters with candles and dim lighting throughout, with all these couples holding hands while they stare lovingly into each other's eyes. The whole thing made me incredibly anxious. I don't really do romance. I don't read romance; I don't watch romance movies. Don't argue with me about musicals being romantic; that's not the main plot point. Plus, have you even heard of *Hamilton*? Not romantic, great musical. You know where I would go if I ate out? McDonald's, maybe Taco Bell. If I was feeling flush and fancy, McCallister's. This restaurant was worlds outside of my experience. I think you're underestimating the amount of non-socializing I had managed to achieve before I met Greg.

"Meg," he said, reaching across the table to grab my hand. I was staring down at the tablecloth. "Meg," he said again, so I looked up at him. "Want to get takeout?"

Relieved, I nodded.

"Wait here," he said. He got up and wove his way

around the tables to the maître d'. I watched them talking; Greg was motioning, the maître d' nodding. Then he wove his way back over to me. He sat down. "Twenty minutes and we can go," he picked my hand back up. "Breathe, Meg. It's just a restaurant, and they're just people. Besides, you could eat all of them for lunch."

I smiled at him. "I definitely could."

The maître d' was by Greg's side, telling him our food was ready if we would just meet the waiter at the door, so Greg led me out, grabbing the bag from the waiter on the way. "Thanks," he said.

Once we were outside, he scooped me up with his free hand, shot us up into the air and landed on a roof somewhere above. The roof itself had more than one level, so we sat at the edge of one of the tiers eating ratatouille out of plastic take out containers, watching the lights in the buildings around us.

Oh, come on, you think you can see the stars in the city? Roof or no roof, no you can't.

"You ever see the movie?" I asked him.

"What movie?"

"*Ratatouille.*"

He gave me a blank look.

I rolled my eyes. "You know, the one about the rat that can cook?"

Greg chuckled. "You mean a kids movie?"

"Hey, it gets deep, it's not just for kids." Plus, it's one of my favorites. What? Don't judge me.

"Mhmm," he said. "Sounds like it's on your level."

"Oh, shut up," I stuck my tongue out at him.

Greg's phone pinged. He had replaced the one that went in the river with him. Virgil has a stash of extras because heroes end up going through phones like candy. I've heard some of the weird ways they've managed to lose or break them. He pulled it out. "Virgil says Ranger gave up about an hour ago."

"Good," I said. "Otherwise, we would have to get a

hotel to avoid listening to that thing buzzing all night."

Greg wrapped an arm around my waist and leaned in, his breath tickling my ear. "We could get a hotel anyway."

"You just don't want to go to the compound in case he comes back and actually hits that buzzer all night long," I teased.

"Mmm," Greg had his lips against my neck. "Maybe I just want to spend time alone with you."

"We're spending time alone together right now."

He huffed, laughing, ribs vibrating against my side. "Meg."

The sound of sirens in the distance, made Greg straighten up.

"What?" I asked him.

"There's a fire. Those are fire trucks."

"You can tell the difference?"

"Yes," he said, but he was distracted, head cocked, listening. He looked around the roof. "I can't leave you here, and we have to go." He looked me in the eye. "Do *not* move from where I put you. I need you to stay out of the way and safe."

"Okay," I said. What would I do in a fire anyway? Fear isn't going to help with that. I would only make the situation worse. And, you know, probably burn to death.

He scooped me up, took off, and headed unerringly for the apartment building that was burning.

He landed me as close to it as he dared. He set me down on the sidewalk. I was in sight of the building and could feel the heat from it even as far back as I was. The firefighters were already at work. The level of noise from the fire - the water spraying out of the hoses, the sirens - was all deafening. The scene in front of the square was chaos; the brick building was full of light from the fire and flashing strobes, the lookie loos on the sidewalks adding to the confusion.

"Stay here," he said and kissed me. Then he was gone, crashing straight through a window, flames belching out in his wake.

I really hope he picked an apartment that was empty to do that to.

Then something happened.

It was like the flames slowed, and then they began to reverse.

The fire fighters had also slowed, like the air had suddenly thickened into molasses, but they weren't going backwards.

I began looking around, because I only knew about one person Virgil had said could manipulate time. I spotted him, across the street and up the sidewalk from me. I darted across the street over to him.

"What the fuck are you doing!" I yelled at him. "Fortress is in there!"

He looked startled. "Shit," he said. Something in the air twisted, and then Greg had slammed the doors open, but because it's Greg they didn't so much open as get thrown, and they came flying at us. "Shit," Ranger repeated, a gust of air around us, and the doors froze, vibrating in the air. He grabbed my shoulders. "Duck!" he yelled, shoving me to the ground, and he leaned his body over mine, his chest pressed to my back, a shield. The doors sped back up, flew over our heads, and crashed into the wall behind us.

Ranger stood up, then grabbed my arm and tried to pull me to my feet. I slapped his hand away, staggering up on my own. "I don't need your help," I snapped at him.

The area in front of the building was full of people covered in soot, and Greg had realized I wasn't where he had left me. I could see the panic on his face.

"Over here!" I bellowed. But he had already spotted me, and he looked pissed. He came up over everyone's heads.

"That is not where I left you," he said. Relief warred with anger in his voice.

"I know, I'm sorry," I said. "Someone was screwing with time while you were inside."

"Oh, thanks for throwing me under the bus here," Ranger said. "I was helping."

"I don't give a shit what you were doing," Greg growled. "Next time, don't." And he swept me up into the air.

∞

He landed on a roof not far from the fire, which I wasn't expecting, I had thought he was going to take us straight back to the compound. He set me down, ran his hands over me. "Are you okay?" he demanded.

"I'm fine," I said. "Not even a scratch."

"Jesus, Meg, you were standing where I threw the doors. If I had hit you with them—" and then his mouth was on mine with an urgency that surprised me. And when I responded he pulled me up against him, settling my legs around his waist, one arm snaked around me.

He slid his free hand under the material of my skirt bunched up between us, and his fingers brushing against my inner thigh made me tremble against him. His lips were on my neck, and then his breath was tickling my ear. "Meg," he said, and my heart fluttered. I turned my head, catching his lips with mine.

His phone rang. We both froze. His forehead was resting against mine. It stopped ringing, and then started again.

Greg sighed and pulled it out, looked at the screen. "Virgil," he said, his breath ragged, "timing."

"Somebody better be fucking dead," I muttered, and waited impatiently because I can't hear any of what's said, like not even that muffled voice noise you can usually get. Greg keeps the call volume on his phone as low as it can go since he can still hear them clearly. He says anything louder, and they might as well be screaming directly in his ear.

But Greg was answering Virgil. "Yeah. Yeah. When? No, I was at the fire, completely missed it."

"Completely missed what?" I demanded.

"Someone hit a jewelry store a couple blocks up from us," Greg said. "No, I was telling Meg. Who else would I be talking to?" A scowl flitted across his face. "He was there. How do you already know that?"

"What?" I asked, getting irritated. "Put him on speaker so I can hear."

Greg chuckled at Virgil's response and pulled the phone away from his face. "Virgil floated a tracker out onto Ranger's bike while he was being so persistent. Says he wants to know where he's going."

"How? From where?"

"From the roof. He can see over the fence from there."

"Huh."

"Where is he now?" Greg asked. "Hmm. So we don't need to go over there," Greg scowled again. "Well maybe you should have bugged him instead. No, Meg isn't dressed for this. I don't want to be dragging her all over town looking for jewelry thieves right now," Greg sighed.

"What?" I demanded again. "Seriously, speaker phone."

"Virgil wants us to go talk to the lead detective, find out what happened. It's not that clown, what's his name, Mason?" He listened. "Uh huh, good. Tell me when Ranger leaves the scene, and we'll go down. No, I don't. I don't like his interest in her."

I leaned back against Greg's arm, crossed my arms. "Don't like whose interest in whom?"

Try looking stern while your legs are still wrapped around someone's waist. Go on, try it. Doesn't work. Especially if their hand is still on your ass.

"Right," Greg said. He hung up, slipped his phone back in his pocket, and put his now free hand on my face. I glared at him.

"Don't like who's interest in whom?" I repeated.

"Ranger's interest in you," he said. "I don't like it. I don't trust it."

"Hmm," I said. I wasn't a fan of it either.

43

"Where were we?" Greg's lips were back on my neck.

"Further up." I closed my eyes, tilting my head to the side.

Greg's phone pinged. Then it pinged again.

"God damn it," Greg muttered, but he pulled his phone back out. "The fucking timing."

"He does it on purpose," I said.

"But how does he know?" Greg was checking the messages. "Ranger's moved on. Come on, let's get this over with. Because then I'm taking you home." He set me down and helped me straighten out the skirt of the dress before he scooped me back up and we took off.

∞

We landed on the sidewalk outside the jewelry store, inside the yellow cordon of tape. It was in the boutique part of town where they made sure there were trees planted in sections of the sidewalk and window boxes with flowers on the front of the stores themselves. We probably weren't far from the store where we got my dress. Not surprisingly there were curious people milling around, a few just off to the side trying to crane their necks to look, one who appeared to be trying to blend into the background so he wouldn't get told to "move-along." The officer beside the door stared at us.

"What?" I said. "Never seen someone fly before?"

He shook his head, still staring mutely.

"Be nice," Greg said, hand on my shoulder, steering me past him into the store.

"Hey, hey!" A woman was striding over to us; dark brown skin, black hair in braids that had been gathered and coiled into a bun at the back of her head. A badge hung around her neck. "You can't be in here! Smith, what are you doing out there?" she yelled around us, trying to use the authority she was projecting to push us back out. The other officers and a CSI tech stopped what they were doing to watch what was going on.

I mean, they probably don't usually get someone in a soot-blackened suit coming into a robbed jewelry store.

"Fortress," Greg said, pointing to himself, then at me. "Vengeance. What happened here?"

"What does it look like happened?" the woman snapped. "I don't need more heroes mucking around in here asking stupid questions."

I snickered.

"Oh, is something funny?" She turned on me.

"Extremely," I said.

Greg sighed. "Vengeance isn't really the heroing type."

The woman's eyes narrowed. "Then what's she doing hanging around with you?"

"Trial period," I said.

The woman's lips twitched. See? I can be funny. "Uh huh," she said at last. "You can't be in here. And I'll tell you what I told the other hero: we don't need your help. It was a simple smash and grab." I assumed she meant that as the colloquial term because nothing was smashed. It looked like the cases had been unlocked.

"What did they take?" Greg asked.

"We don't know yet. We're waiting on the owner to come down and give us an inventory check. But like I said, we don't need your help. We've got it covered."

"Security tapes?" Greg asked.

"Already on their way to the station for review. Again, don't need help."

Greg pulled a card out of his pocket and held it out to the detective. "If you do need our help," he said.

She slipped it into her pocket. "I doubt we will."

Greg waited. Finally, she sighed, pulled out one of her own business cards and handed it over. Greg looked it over and nodded. "Detective White." He steered me back outside and pulled me against him. Officer Smith was still staring at us.

"What?" I said.

Greg sighed, and then took us into the air.

CHAPTER FOUR

Sand, the sea and an olive grove. The feel of grass pricking my feet. Bark, rough under my fingers and the palms of my hands.

A message on the wind.

∞

I heard Greg grumbling on the bed next to me. I raised my head, blinking sleep out of my eyes, but the vague sense of a dream that wasn't a dream lingered. "What?" I asked him.

"Shhh," he said, kissing my shoulder. "Go back to sleep." He got up.

Well, now I was awake. "Where are you going?"

"Someone's at the callbox again. Virgil's going to have a fit." He headed out of the bedroom, closing the door behind him. I sighed, slipped out of bed, and got dressed. I pulled open the door to follow him down the hallway. He had already reached the security room before I had come out, and I could hear him and Virgil arguing in hushed voices.

"What's up?" I asked, leaning against the frame, instead of just eavesdropping. Of course, I eavesdrop. Just in case they're talking about things they're not planning on telling me about.

"Ranger is back," Virgil sounded incredibly miffed about it.

Greg was leaning back against the control board. "I still say I should go out and run him off."

"And I think we should at least hear him out first," Virgil said. "I want to know why he's so focused on this."

Greg was grinding his teeth. "Stop that," I said. "Jesus, just see what he wants and then tell him to go away. It's not like it's hard."

"Thank you, Meg," Virgil said, and then turned and looked pointedly at Greg. He stepped out of the way of the board. Virgil reached over and hit the intercom. "Now what?" he snapped. I love listening to Virgil sound irritated when it's not directed at me. Pretty sure he could give any of the great actors a run for their money. It was why his mood around Greg and me had been so mercurial when we first met. He was pushing me off balance on purpose. You know, I never apologized for attacking him that one time. I should get around to that.

"Let me talk to Vengeance," Ranger demanded.

"Why should I do that?" Virgil asked.

"I want to know why I don't affect her!"

Virgil muted the mic and looked at me.

"Wow," I said. "The ego on him."

He unmuted. "She says you're nowhere near as cute as you think you are," Virgil said. I snorted.

There was a pause. "But she still thinks I'm cute, right?" Ranger's tone sounded amused. Now I wasn't laughing.

"Okay, I'm hanging up now," Virgil said.

"Wait! Why doesn't my power affect her? Why are you people so difficult?"

"Hmm, not used to hearing no very often, are you?" Virgil said.

There was another pause. Then, warily, "If I tell you no, I'm not, will you still let me in?"

"I don't recall saying I would let you in the first place."

Greg was still grinding his teeth. "I say we don't let him in regardless."

Virgil muted the mic again. "I think we should find out why the two of them can't seem to affect each other. It could give us more information about what Meg can do."

"The figures can still rip into him," I said.

I could see Virgil's shoulders tense, and he turned to fix his eyes on me. I felt like I needed to back up. "One, when did you find that out, and two, when were you going to tell me?"

"Hello?" came Ranger's voice.

Virgil unmuted. "I'm thinking about it." He hit the mute again. "Well, Meg?"

I cleared my throat. "At the bank, one of them snagged his jacket. And then when we got home and the news..."

"You forgot," Virgil sighed. I nodded, eyes on the floor. "Okay," he said. "Any other times? What about in the alleys when you were with Susan?"

"Yes. He shoved me into a wall, and they got him then too."

"He did what?" Greg growled.

"Well, he chased me into a dead end," I paused. "That just makes it sound worse, doesn't it?"

Greg shoved his hair back out of his face. "Yes, it does. I hope you tore a chunk out of him."

"I might have," I admitted. "If it makes you feel any better, I don't think he realized it was me he was chasing. At least, not until he had me pinned."

"That's not helping."

"If you two are done," Virgil said, "I think we're going to have to let him in to find out exactly what this means."

Greg sighed. "Fine."

They both looked at me. "Fine," I said. "But don't blame me if all your stuff gets ruined again."

Virgil chuckled, then unmuted the mic. "I'm opening the gate. You can sit outside until I'm ready to open the doors." He hung up and then hit the button for the gate. We watched Ranger hop onto his bike and ride it up the driveway. He stopped in front of the steps, dismounted, and then waited, sitting sideways on it, leaning forward, elbows on his knees.

"So," Virgil said, "which one of us volunteers to go say hello?"

"Not it," I said.

∞

Virgil ended up being the one to go let him in the building itself. Greg could hear every word they were saying because Virgil had left the doors open, and he didn't look like he appreciated what was being said because he was scowling again.

"What?" I hissed at him. He waved a hand at me. I heard footsteps coming down, the heavy tread of steel toed boots. Those definitely weren't Virgil's; his were combat. I knew because he had told me.

Ranger appeared at the bottom of the stairs. He swept the room with his eyes and then immediately headed in my direction.

Greg stepped into his path. Ranger stopped. He leaned to one side to lock eyes with me. "You want to call off your attack dog?"

"No," I said, from the arm of the chair I was half sitting and half leaning on. If Greg was planting himself in the way like that, he had his reasons, and we would discuss it in private. In public against an unknown, I'm straight up sticking by his side. Or out of it altogether.

Virgil sailed in. "One of these days you're going to do that to one of my chairs, and it'll flip on you."

"Only because you'd flip it," I said.

"Touché," Virgil said. He steered around both Ranger and Greg, neither of whom had moved. "You know you can sit down, right?"

"I would, but someone's blocking the room," Ranger

said.

"Greg," Virgil said. Ah, so Virgil wasn't going to poke at Greg while we had a guest. I flashed Virgil a small smile. He smiled back at me. Greg still hadn't moved.

"Okay," Ranger said. "Well, I'm going to go sit down." He started to step around Greg's left towards the side of the room I was on. Greg matched his movement. Ranger squared up against him. "Don't test me."

"Or you'll what?" Greg asked.

"Boys," Virgil called, "as entertaining as this is, you're going to try Meg's patience, and we know how she gets."

Ranger clicked his tongue. "Meg, huh?"

"Okay," I said. "I'm out. Call me when you all grow up." Calling everyone out isn't the same as calling just Greg out.

"Excuse me," Ranger said, "but you set the attack dog first."

"Oh no," Virgil said, "he does that all on his own. Sensitive type." Greg turned his head enough to shoot Virgil a glare. Ranger tried to step around him on my side again, and Greg's arm shot out, blocking him.

Greg pointed to his right. "Couches are over there," he told Ranger. They stood there for another moment before Ranger stepped backwards towards the couches, hands up in a conciliatory gesture, but there was a smirk on his face.

I'm not sure where Ranger thought he was going to go if he came over to me, since the chair I was leaning against was set to one side of the entertainment center and TV remnants, so other than the floor, it was the only available seating. Unless he was going to try and make me give up my seat, and that wasn't happening.

Once he reached the couches, Ranger didn't sit. He stood, legs braced, arms crossed, mimicking Greg's stance, still smirking, a challenge in his eyes. Inwardly, I scoffed: he's the idiot who walked into the lion's den, and the bravado was getting old.

Virgil motioned impatiently at the seating. "Would everyone please sit down, and we can discuss this like adults?"

"That might be asking a bit much," I muttered, but I shifted position so that I was seated in the chair itself rather than on the arm. Greg took up a standing position next to and slightly behind me; arms crossed, he leaned back against the available wall.

Virgil pointed at me. "Stop being a bad influence."

"I'm sitting!" I protested.

"You know exactly what I mean," Virgil said. He turned his attention to Ranger. "There's a couch. Sit."

Ranger did as he was told, sitting on the couch with legs spread, leaning back into the cushions, both arms flung across the back. "What happened to your TV?" he asked. Virgil still hadn't replaced the one I broke.

"Meg did," Virgil said.

"Thought your name was Vengeance," Ranger said.

"Vengeance is Meg's public name. Consider yourself privileged," Virgil told him. Ranger just grunted. Virgil steepled his fingers and watched Ranger for a moment. "So, explain what you mean by Meg doesn't seem to be affected by your power."

"She doesn't stop, or reverse, or react to it. She just – she keeps going, with the freaky demon shit."

"Hmm," Virgil said. "Meg? Did you notice anything? Were you using your power every time he interacted with you?"

"I only used them on her in the alley," Ranger clarified. He noticed the glare Greg was giving him. "Look, I wouldn't have done it normally, but I didn't realize who she was until after I hit her, and then the second time was because of the first."

"What about at the fire?" Greg asked, moving past the subject, although I could hear the anger in his tone.

"No, didn't try it on her at all. It's got a perimeter effect. I can keep it within just that circle, so I didn't stretch it to include her." He thought for a minute. "Just the doors you threw."

Greg came off the wall.

"Greg," Virgil and I said at the same time. Greg hesitated, settled a hand on my shoulder. I reached back, wiggling my fingers into his so they were interlaced. The tension around him vanished. There's something about when I show him the same casual affection he shows me that makes him relax. Even his usual coiled energy isn't quite as tight.

Ranger was watching us, the look on his face considering.

Virgil was also considering, but his gaze included Ranger. "I think," he said slowly, "that we may want to test this."

"Test what?" Ranger asked.

"You also seem, unaffected, at least in part, by Meg's power."

"You mean she can do more than slice people up? I mean, that's impressive enough, I've got a scar from that."

Virgil snorted. "You didn't notice at the bank?"

"What, you mean where everyone freaked out and ran away from her? I figured that was because of the, what are they? They look like shadows."

"Meg's power is fear. Although, it's grown in scope," Virgil said.

"Torment," I said. Because that was part of what the whispers and figures wanted. But none of us mentioned he could see them because he had powers. Look, we're operating on need to know, and right now, he doesn't need to know.

"That's—" Ranger paused. "so, are you actually a demon?"

"The closest comparison is a Fury," Virgil said.

"If I knew what that meant, that word might tell me something," Ranger said. "Is she human or not?"

"She," I said, "is right here and can answer for herself. And I am human, thank you very much."

"Look, I don't deal with this kind of stuff usually. I keep to the simple stuff: save lives, stop robberies, get laid," he winked at me. The whispers were in my ear and I could feel Greg tense again, and I knew it wasn't entirely due to Ranger. I let the whispers go.

Yeah, I still gotta work on the whole self-control thing.

Virgil got up, crossed the room, pulled a book off the bookcases, and tossed it into Ranger's lap, who started. "Read that," Virgil said. "It'll at least give you a vague idea of what Meg's power is like. Can I see you two in the kitchen?"

Greg and I followed Virgil out. Ranger craned his neck to watch us. "You guys going to bring back refreshments?"

Virgil closed the kitchen door with a snap. "As much as I don't like it, I think we're going to need him to stay here until we can figure out exactly what his level of immunity is.'"

"Why do we even need to know that?" I asked. "We know there's immunity. Isn't that enough?"

"No. If anyone else can demonstrate an ability like that, I want to be able to predict how much. What happens if we run into someone who's immune to the fear and you're their target?"

"We already know he didn't react to the fear at all," I argued.

"How much of it were you pulling on Meg?"

I paused. "Just, the aura, the whispers stayed right against me. Usually that's enough to get people to run."

"Expand it. I want to know how far out before he notices it, if at all. And I want to know how much of his power isn't affecting you."

I made a frustrated noise. Greg wrapped an arm around my waist. "I don't like it either," he told me, "but Virgil's right. We need to know."

"If you say no, Meg, we won't make you. But I think it would be the wrong choice," Virgil said.

"I'd like to see you try and make me do anything," I said.

"Please, Meg," Greg said. "Anything we learn can only help keep you protected."

I was silent for a long moment. If it had been anyone

but Greg asking me to protect myself, I would've ignored them. Well, maybe I wouldn't have ignored Virgil, but he wasn't the one who's feelings I was considering on the matter, because Virgil's were based in what would be entirely practical.

"Okay," I said. "But if he pisses me off, I'm not responsible for what happens."

∞

Virgil headed outside to set up for observation. The only other place in the compound with enough room would have been in his garage, and he wasn't risking his cars.

Greg made breakfast, because while we didn't know, or honestly care, about Ranger, the rest of us hadn't eaten yet. I made the coffee because I manage to burn even boiled eggs.

Look, don't ask how I managed to survive on my own for so long. I ate a lot of prepackaged, canned and frozen foods.

Since Greg was the one cooking, the omelets he made were meat free, but he packed in a ton of veggies and cheese. He set one aside for Virgil and then ate the half of mine I didn't finish.

I took the moment to talk to him. "You know I can kick his ass on my own, right?"

Greg looked up from my omelet. "I know."

"So, let me," I said. "If I need an assist, I'll tell you."

"Okay," he said, and he gave me a kiss and went back to his food. That was too easy; it most definitely wasn't going to be the end of it. Probably because he knew I would murder someone before I asked for help.

We were still sitting at the kitchen island drinking coffee when Ranger wandered in. He came around the island so he was facing us and tossed Virgil's book onto the counter. He leaned back against the counter and cabinets behind him. "Nice of you to offer me some," he said.

Greg grunted and pointed behind him. "Pot and mugs are behind you."

"Oh, I don't want any. Just making a point," he said, looking at me. "He always like this?"

"You'll have to be more specific," I said.

He narrowed his eyes at me. "Specific about what?"

"Which he and what said he is like."

Greg chuckled. "Virgil's rubbing off on you."

"I'm sorry, but I'm pretty sure the smart-ass comments have always been part of my charm."

"Smart ass, yes, evasive maneuvers not so much."

"Hmm," I said. Because I was pretty sure he was wrong.

Ranger continued to watch us. The tension in the room was slowly rising.

And you already know I hate silence. "You have a problem?" I asked him.

"You don't seem the type to go for muscle heads," he said.

I opened my mouth to snap back a retort, but Greg chuckled. "Haven't heard that one before."

"I'm not surprised you don't remember; I bet not much registers in that skull," Ranger sneered.

I started to open my mouth again, but Greg wrapped an arm around my waist and kissed the side of my forehead. I leaned into him; I was getting used to his casual affection with me, and I wasn't above straight up encouraging it in front of someone whose interest I didn't want. See, I knew our talk wasn't over.

I'm not sure Ranger's eyes could narrow any further without being shut.

Virgil chose that moment to come into the kitchen. "Where's breakfast?" he asked. Greg pointed at the fridge. Virgil pulled his plate out and stuck it in the microwave.

Greg made a slightly strangled noise. "At least use the oven to reheat that."

"No," Virgil said. "I'm hungry now." He stopped next to Ranger, who was in the way of the coffee pot. "Move or I will make you." Ranger side stepped, and Virgil helped himself to a mug and coffee. The microwave beeped. Virgil grabbed his plate and brought it and his mug over to my other side. He left me space, though. Guess he figured Greg was tense enough.

Ranger continued to watch us silently, and the silence was making me itch. I slid off my stool.

"I'll be outside," I said. Ranger started to straighten up.

"Tell me about what you can do," Virgil said, and while Ranger was distracted, I slipped out of the kitchen, through the living room and up the stairs. I left the doors open; I wouldn't have been able to open them if I closed them behind me anyway.

I sat down on the steps, eyeing Ranger's bike. Would he know who did it if it just happened to be knocked over on its side when he came out? Greg might not care about the snide comments he was making, but I sure did.

What? I get to protect myself and what's mine. Me telling Greg to let me handle myself is absolutely not the same. Did you just accuse me of being a hypocrite? Okay, fine, I'll own it.

Greg sat down next to me. "I know what you're thinking, and I won't tell. Virgil might though."

I laughed. "He wouldn't."

"He wouldn't," Greg agreed. He slung an arm over my shoulders. "Don't worry about him trying to insult me. I don't give a shit what he thinks about me."

"Then why were you—" I paused, trying to think of the best way to ask the question without sounding like I was accusing him of something. But if there was going to be constant running of interference, we were going to have to have another talk about how I could handle it on my own. I wasn't helpless, and I didn't need Greg jumping between us every time Ranger looked in my direction. I could get him to back down on my own. Like I've said, I can rescue myself.

Greg was silent next to me, and I still hadn't finished my thought, but he spoke up before I could. "I don't like the – the read I'm getting on him," he admitted and scrubbed at his face. "Ever since Bolt, I just don't want to misjudge like that again—" he took a breath, but then stayed silent, and I felt like there was something left unsaid.

Footsteps sounded behind us, so I didn't get to ask, because Virgil and Ranger had come outside with us.

"Meg, if you're ready, we're set up for the usual spot," Virgil said.

I hopped up and headed for the grass beyond the drive. My shoulders felt cold without Greg's arm around them. Ranger followed me. I stopped, and he had to dodge around me to avoid a collision.

"Little warning would've been nice," he said.

He was still standing next to me, and I flicked my eyes over at him. "You're going to want to back up."

Virgil called out, "Step out about five feet to your right, Ranger. Meg, expand it slowly."

I gave Ranger a minute to move away from me. Side note: five feet is not as much distance as you would think, which might be why Virgil was pushing so hard for me to get the range larger than ten, he wanted me to be able to clear out a building without having to go room by room. But the figures can't go through walls anyway, so that might not be realistic. They're too - solid? - would be the closest word for that. Even though they're solid enough they can't go through walls, they can't catch a bullet for me, they're too amorphous for that. What? They're capricious. I don't make the rules.

I called to the whispers, and they came, figures brushing against my back and legs, shadows pooling at my feet, and I told them what to do. They swirled forward, circling around me, eddying like sharks in the water. Ranger watched them warily but didn't react otherwise.

"Anything?" Virgil called.

"I mean, I see them. I'm supposed to see them, right?" Ranger asked.

Yes, the whispers laughed.

"Yes," Virgil said. "Meg, expand it again. We're going to go foot by foot so not much."

The figures moved forward, flowing through the air. Rustling the grass with their long fingers. The shadows expanded, rippling over the ground.

Ranger took a step back from them.

"Anything?" Virgil asked.

Ranger shook his head. "I feel normal other than the fact that I don't want to get touched by one of those things again." Normal, human caution.

"Again," Virgil commanded.

Seven feet. Eight feet.

Each time Ranger just took a step back and didn't seem bothered other than when the figures tried to reach out at him.

At ten feet they settled into a circle around me, silent sentinels of smoke and ink. They stopped moving, the whispers floating in the air, pressing on my ears.

"Whoa," Ranger said, stepping forward to take a closer look.

The figures rushed to converge on him, and he took a hurried stumbling step back. "Shit!"

He was out of reach, and they flowed back outward into the circle around me.

"Meg?" Virgil asked cautiously.

"Wasn't me!" I snapped. "Guard mode, remember?"

"Hmm," grunted Virgil.

"Excuse me?" Ranger demanded. "Does she not have control over her own power?"

"Taking the fifth," said Virgil.

"What kind of operation are you running here?" Ranger squared off facing Virgil. "You're letting a ticking timebomb wander around the city with little to no oversight?"

Rude. And not true. I do so have oversight. Of myself.

Okay, yeah, Greg and Virgil keep an eye on me too.

"We don't owe you any kind of explanation as to how Meg's power works," Virgil said steadily. He was doing his "teacher tone" again. "You came to us, you harassed us. If you want to know why your power doesn't work on her, you'll shut up and wait until we trust you enough to give you an explanation."

Through the figures I could see Ranger's fists had clenched at his side, but he didn't say anything. He just turned to face me again.

"Are we ready? Good. Okay, Meg, keep them out where they are. We're going to tighten it up bit by bit. Ranger," Virgil paused and waited until Ranger acknowledged him with a jerk of his head, "I want you to try and slow her. You said it just seems to blow back off her right?"

"Yes," Ranger said.

"Okay, when you're ready, hit her."

There was a gust of air. And then nothing happened. We stood there, and I don't know about Ranger, but I felt kind of silly waiting for something that wasn't working.

Ranger sighed. "Can you make them back up, Meg?"

"Oh, did you do it already?" Virgil asked.

I snorted, one hand on my mouth. I knew that tone Virgil was using.

"Yes, I did it already," Ranger snapped.

The whispers giggled in my ear. For something made of fear itself, they sure seemed to like it when I was laughing.

"Meg?" Virgil said. I cleared my throat and pulled the figures back toward me. "Okay, again!" Virgil called.

And back we went, shadows melting back toward me, the figures pulling in, sometimes leaving furrows in the ground as they went. Each time Ranger tried to use his power on me there was a gust of air and nothing else.

He was getting frustrated. "This doesn't explain why it doesn't work!"

"Testing theories takes time and effort," Virgil said calmly, still surveying. The whispers and figures were against me now, brushing along my skin, ruffling my hair, shadows gathered at my legs. "Meg, can you let them go? I want to see if you're still immune when you're not using your power."

I nodded and told the whispers to go. They sighed and went, and the unease in the air disappeared. "Okay," I said. "Clear."

Virgil motioned at Ranger, who turned back to me, and shook out his hands, and this time when the gust of air hit me, something happened.

The air around me thickened, I could feel my heart in my chest, slow, steady, and when I tried to step forward it was like trying to wade through water. It was as if the air had congealed in my lungs, thick and viscous, and my chest went tight, the pressure of it pushing in against me. The figures boiled forward, breaking the heaviness around me, and then they were gone, but because I had been trying to move, my body continued forward, it's momentum suddenly sped up. I staggered, arms out, but Ranger caught me before I could fall.

"Whoa there, little lady," he said.

The whispers shrieked, the figures billowing, and they slammed him into the ground. He gave a startled scream as they tore into his jacket. I could hear Virgil swearing in the background, and Ranger disappeared from my view as Virgil yanked him out of reach.

I was on my knees, struggling to breathe. The figures and shadows were rushing through the air, and then they withdrew, but I hadn't told them to go. Greg's arms were around me, pulling me into him. I was shaking and shivering, my heart hammering in my chest.

"Meg, Meg," he said, his voice in my ear. "Shhhh, it's okay, you're safe here. Red Eye's dead, and you're safe here." I burst into tears, hiding my face in his chest. His arms tightened around me.

Virgil cleared his throat. "I think we're done for today."

CHAPTER FIVE

Greg had insisted on settling me on a stool in the kitchen and told Ranger to "stay the fuck out under pain of death." He set a mug in front of me, the liquid in it steaming.

"What is this?" I asked.

"Chamomile tea. My mom used to make it for us whenever one of us was upset."

I perked up. "Us? You didn't tell me you have siblings. How many? Brothers? Sisters?"

"Two. Brothers. And I hadn't told you because we don't talk much. They're busy with their own lives," he said as he settled on the stool next to me. "I'd like you to meet my mom, though."

"What about your dad?" I asked, switching subjects because I didn't know if I was ready for that.

He shrugged. "He left when I was little. Don't know where he is."

"Oh." Well, I knew about asshole parents.

Okay, maybe it's unfair to put all the blame on my parents. They were good parents up until I was sixteen, and I guess it's kind of hard to forgive your daughter for murdering a houseful of people, even if it wasn't intentional. I'm still pissed they went ahead with being interviewed by the news, though.

I wasn't sure if the story had aired, or when, if it had.

Probably for the best. I didn't really want to know what they had to say about or to me.

Something was niggling at the back of my mind. I hadn't told Greg that Red Eye had kept calling me little lady. But I had told Virgil.

"How'd you know?" I demanded, turning to face him.

He looked caught. He cleared his throat. "The lab and kitchen share a wall."

Which meant he had heard the entire thing when Virgil had interviewed me following Red Eye's capture and subsequent torture of me. I looked away from him, down at my tea. I pushed it away.

"Meg, I'm sorry, I know you're mad—"

"Yes, I'm fucking mad!" I got off the stool. "I didn't want you to know, I didn't want to—" but what exactly I didn't want I wasn't sure. I just knew I hadn't felt ready to tell him anything of what had happened. It had been hard enough going through it again with Virgil, and Virgil had kept it clinical. I couldn't handle the emotions it would have brought up telling the story to Greg.

I gave up on my tirade and stormed out of the kitchen, stomping down to our room and slammed the door behind me. And then I locked it. It would've been a futile gesture, what with his super strength, but I knew Greg, and he would respect the action behind it. Because I wasn't coming out until I was ready to talk to him.

∞

Someone was knocking on the door. "GO AWAY!" I yelled.

There was a pause. "You know I can just unlock it," Virgil said, his voice muffled by the wood.

I muttered, slid off the bed, unlocked and opened the door a crack. "What do you want?"

"To talk."

"Well, I don't want to talk."

"I surmised that."

"Then why are you still here?"

"Because I don't care that you don't want to talk," Virgil said, "and I will stand here until you let me in."

I threw my hands up and stepped away from the door. "Fine."

"Thank you," Virgil said, slipping in and closing the door behind him. Then he stood there, leaning against it.

I rolled my eyes, perched on the edge of the bed. "Are you going to talk?"

"I would like to do more testing. It would appear it's your power that's immune to Ranger's."

"I thought you were here to talk to me about Greg."

"Oh no, I'm not getting in the middle of that. His eavesdropping is between the two of you. Although I suppose I should share that he would've heard at least part of it no matter where he went in this compound," he cut me off before I could fully open my mouth, "*and* I didn't mention it to you at the time because I knew pulling the tale out of you would be difficult enough. So you can lay part of the blame on me."

Silence. He waited, watching me.

"What kind of testing?" I grumbled. If I had been thinking logically at the time or now, I would've known that Greg would have been able to hear everything I said. And I should've known that Virgil would also know that. Never say I let logic get in the way of my emotions.

"I want Ranger to hit you with his power, and when he does that, you use yours to see if it breaks again like it did earlier today."

"And how many times are we going to do that?"

"Until I'm satisfied that I have an answer."

"Fine."

"We'll take a break for the rest of the day and get started again in the morning. I want to make sure we don't have a repeat of earlier. Ranger is still shedding sticks and leaves from when I got him out of your way."

"Where'd you throw him?"

"The bushes. It was the softest landing spot available."

I snorted. It meant Virgil had literally thrown him halfway across the grounds. Tossing Ranger that far had been entirely unnecessary to get him out of my range.

Virgil turned and cracked open the door. Sighed. Closed it. "Meg, do you want company, or are you still in a mood?"

"Greg's out there, isn't he?"

"Hmm, technically he's been hovering since you locked him out."

"I can hear you," Greg's voice said. Of course he would.

I flopped backwards onto the bed. "You can leave it open." I heard the door open, footsteps trading places, the door closed. I stared at the canopy of the bed and felt the mattress depress when Greg sat down next to me. He leaned over me so I was looking him in the eye.

"I'm sorry," he said.

"Hmm," I said. "Maybe we should stop doing things we have to apologize to each other for."

He chuckled. "I don't know that you're capable of doing that."

I stuck my tongue out at him.

He flopped down next to me; the mattress springs groaned. He slid an arm under me, and pulled me to him. I cuddled up against him, settling my head on his shoulder.

"I shouldn't have listened," he said. "It's not an excuse, but I was scared for you, and I had no way to help you. And I thought if I knew—" he sighed. "Well, I didn't end up with a way to help you. And I'm sorry."

We were silent, and for once I just let it stretch.

∞

Eventually Virgil had Ranger move his bike down to the

garage. Greg went down there with them because Virgil wanted him to hold the Hummer up while he checked something.

I suspected it was actually to show Ranger just what he was dealing with when it came to Greg and the damage he could do. Guess Greg isn't the only one feeling territorial right now.

I had taken the opportunity to come out of our room and browse Virgil's books. I mean, what else was I going to do for entertainment? The TV was still broken. Bolt was right; he did have a lot of romance novels. I paused on *Lust and Lechery*. Geez, Virgil, what kind of bodice rippers are you into? I had moved further down and was perusing the number of books he had on classic cars when I heard footsteps come in. Their owner came up and leaned against the bookcase next to me; out of the corner of my eye I caught sight of boots and leather. I kept my eyes focused on the books in front of me.

"Hey," Ranger said.

"What do you want?"

"I don't know what I did to freak you out exactly."

"Then maybe you shouldn't be talking to me so you can make sure you don't do it again."

Silence for a moment. "You have a problem with me?"

"I have a problem with anyone who gets into my space when they're not wanted," I snapped. And to be honest, the space I need between other people and me has gotten a lot bigger ever since Red Eye. My temper was shorter, and apparently, I had a trigger. I would say I've needed therapy since high school, but one, where would I find a therapist who could deal with that, and two, I probably wouldn't go even if I could find one.

What? Some of us choose the path of struggling on our own rather than getting treatment. Don't judge me. And other heroes, the ones who could understand what I had done, the effect it had on a person, they don't generally go into therapy as a career path. The clientele pool is too small, so we only have each other to talk to. A normal therapist isn't equipped for this kind of shit anyway.

Surprisingly, Ranger backed up, and that was enough to make me turn to look at him.

"Oh, I've got your attention now?" he asked.

"Had," I said and turned back to the books. If he was going to be snarky, he better be ready to get as good as he gave.

"Are you always this prickly?"

"I've been told it's my best feature." I mean, I'm just downright delightful, wouldn't you agree? Don't answer that.

He snorted. "I would hate to see your worst."

"Then why are you talking to me?"

"You," he started, then paused. "I don't get you."

"Not many people do." Although honestly, what is there to get? I pulled a book at random off the shelf. I started to turn, and he caught my arm. "Let go of me," I said, the whispers sighing in my ears.

"How long have you and the attack dog been a thing?" he asked, his hand still on me.

"I don't see how that's any of your business." I jerked my arm away.

"Is it serious?"

"Also none of your business."

"I don't think it's serious."

"And what would give you that impression? The whole five minutes you've known us?" I moved away from him and headed for a chair on the opposite side of the room.

"Well, see, most of the time when a relationship is serious, the girl I'm talking to loves to spill the details, which is nice; it lets me know I don't have a chance. But you, you're pretty close-lipped," he was following me to the chair, so I switched tactics, turning on my heel so that he had to come to a stop or run into me. He did the smart thing and took a step back, putting space between us. I had the book up, pressed against my chest like it was a shield.

"I don't see how that has any relevance," I said.

"Well, I think it means I have a chance."

I rolled my eyes. "You have, literally, no chance."

"Yeah? Then answer the question. Is it serious?"

"You have no chance *is* the answer." Even if I didn't have Greg, he would have no chance. I'm dramatic enough all on my own. I don't need some showboating bad boy biker hero type in my life.

"Yeah, so basically I do."

"No, you don't—" I was snapping at him when he held up a hand.

"Shush," he said. His head was tilted like he was trying to hear something, his eyes distant.

"Don't shush me."

He looked up. "I need to go. We need to go." He snagged my elbow, stepping toward the door as I jerked my arm away.

"Go where?" I asked suspiciously.

"There's," he was snapping his fingers, "tables in—"

"Tables in what?"

"We have to go or people are going to die." He darted past me for Virgil's room, where the entrance to the garage was.

Maybe he should have led with that. I dropped the book and followed him, both of us racing past the sliding bookcase and down the stairs.

"We need to go! Something's going to go down," Ranger was yelling as we came out into the garage.

Virgil and Greg were turning from the car they had been leaning over.

"Going down where?" Virgil asked.

"City," Ranger paused, his head tilted again, "some gala or something." He was snapping his fingers again. "Damn it, some, some sort of medical charity? It's not coming in clear enough."

"When? How long do we have?" Virgil asked.

"I can't, agh, damn it. I can't tell."

"Greg, take Meg. Go ahead of us, we'll catch up. Ranger, in the Cobra. I'm driving. Try for more detail on the way."

Greg snatched me up, and we were up and out of the tunnel before the ramp had finished opening. Below us I saw Virgil's car come leaping out before the compound was lost below the low-hanging clouds and retreating light of the setting sun.

∞

Greg landed us on top of a building in the middle of downtown. He called Virgil as soon as he had set me down. "Any more details coming through? But which building? Have you called—" A pause as he listened. "If he can't give you the name of the building, can he give you details? Does he even know what architecture means?" Greg was listening again. I waited, impatient. "That sounds like the Sung building. No, no, Meg and I are going. If they're not hosting anything, I'll call you back," he hung up.

He scooped me back up and took off, and we went almost straight down. I hid my face, clinging to his neck. He landed on the sidewalk. There were startled exclamations around us, and I realized we were surrounded by men and women in black tie. They were very glittery. Like, crazy amounts of sparkle in terms of jewelry. Greg set me down and started leading me up the steps to the doors, steering me around a woman with peacock feathers bobbing in her hair and lining the neckline of her gown. The eyes in the feathers winked at me in the lights.

"Excuse us," Greg said. He pulled out his phone, tapped out a quick message, and put it away. We were at the doors, and the man standing there turned his nose up.

"This is a *private* event," he said.

"We need to get inside and speak to security," Greg told him.

"That's not going to happen unless you can present invitations. And per the invitation, this event is black tie *only*."

"I'm Fortress, this is Vengeance, and it is urgent that we come inside. We've been alerted—"

"I don't care if you're the Pope, you're not coming in."

"Why are we arguing with him?" I hissed. The whispers sighed in my ears, figures skittering up the decorative columns on either side of the doors. The man at the door did a double take and started to back away from me.

"Vengeance," Greg snapped at me. I let the whispers go. I was slipping, exposing Greg to the fear when he was too close to me. I needed to get better control. "Recon first," Greg said more calmly. "We can't just go charging in half-cocked."

"That sounds strangely familiar," I said.

"Good advice I got once," he said. He loomed over the man at the door. "You will let us in, and you will let us speak to security or Vengeance is going to cause a scene, and you don't want that." See, even Greg isn't above taking advantage of the influence the compulsion I put out gives us.

The man cleared his throat, his eyes fastened on me. "Okay, security is down the hall to the right. But I didn't let you in."

"Thank you," Greg said sharply, and he steered me around the apparent gatekeeper.

Inside the lobby there were people climbing another set of stairs. I could hear strains of music coming from the room above us, but Greg was headed down to the right, and I followed him, away from the sparkling chandeliers and soaring interior space toward the open doorway of a long hall.

We hadn't gone more than a few steps when the screaming started. Greg did an about face and snatched me up. We were at the top of the stairs before I could orient myself. He set me down.

"Get them evacuated," he told me, and then he was gone, headed into the room the screams were coming from. People were streaming out, screaming, and over the sounds of their screams I could hear crashing, the tinkling of breaking glass. And something roared.

People had slowed, pausing to turn and stare back at whatever was happening.

"Oh for – RUN!" I yelled at them, calling the whispers, figures and shadows swirling around me.

They ran.

I waited by the entrance long enough to make sure no one else was coming out and then chased the people still stupid enough to linger the rest of the way down the stairs.

Once I had terrified the remaining people into exiting through the front doors, I ran back up the stairs, taking them two at a time. There was roaring and crashing still coming from what a sign outside declared Ballroom 1, and apparently I was headed in there.

Well, that was my plan until I heard the squeaking and scurrying. I turned.

Have you ever seen *The Princess Bride*? You know the part where they're in the Fire Swamp, and Wesley says there's no such thing as Rodents of Unusual Size? And turns out he's wrong?

They were about that size.

Unlike ROUSs, they didn't have fur. They were naked, pink-skinned, but rotten-looking. Sore and bleeding, pieces of flesh were sloughing off their legs and tails. And they and their nasty, long front teeth were headed straight for me.

I peddled back from them, the whispers roaring in my ears, figures billowing out, shadows spreading across the floor, and they slammed into the horde of giant zombie rats. The rats burst, blood and guts spilling out in a rusty red wave. The smell of putrid meat made me gag.

The figures and shadows came back to me, curling around my waist and legs, up along my shoulders, while I waited to see if there were more of the rats.

Nothing moved, but the crashing was still happening.

And I did not want to wade through what was left of the rats to get to the doors.

Maybe the ballroom had more than one entrance?

I turned and headed up the hallway that was on the right and around the corner. Lo and behold, through another open set of double doors to my left, and I could hear crashing going on inside. It sounded like someone was throwing tables.

How have they not run out of tables by this point? How many people were they expecting at this thing?

I went to head through the doors, and standing there was a man: the kind who tended to be non-descript, brown hair, brown eyes, the kind of features you see on so many people they tend to all blur together. He turned, startled by my entrance. Behind him I could see Greg fighting what looked like an immensely huge humanoid rat. And I mean *immense*; it towered over him, and looked like it had been raised on a steroid only diet. At least this one didn't look like a zombie.

It's the little things.

But what ended up catching my full attention was the pistol in the man's hands, and he was shaking because the whispers, figures and shadows were still curling around me.

I needed to make a decision. Because I wasn't dressed for this. And getting shot was not on my to do list for the day.

I backed up a bit, hands up, palms out. "Oookay, let's just put the gun down."

"No," he said. I could hear the tremor in his voice.

"How about," I was working hard to sound friendly and harmless, trying to get the whispers to back off and go, but they weren't listening to me. "How about I just get out of your way so you can leave? No one needs to get hurt."

I was also trying not to attract Greg's attention. If I sounded panicked, if he could hear my heart start to race, he was going to leave off his fight with the thing, and I didn't think we wanted a giant rat free to run around the city.

The man seemed to be thinking it over.

Now, you might be asking why I didn't just attack him. One, I didn't know who he was. He could be a cop, which was currently my guess because the way he was handling that pistol meant he knew his way around firearms, and two, while I've attacked people with guns before, we all know how that could turn out. I don't want to be a casualty for someone else's dumbass decisions.

Oh, damn it. I'd been doing hero shit without realizing it. No wonder the heroes wouldn't leave me alone.

"Fine," he finally said, after what felt like eons. The whispers and I were getting impatient. "You," he motioned at me with the pistol, "will back the fuck up, up against the wall. And I will leave."

"Absolutely," I said, backing out of the doors, until my back bumped into the wall across the hallway. The man followed me, keeping the pistol pointed at my chest. See, center mass! Probably a cop, like I said. He edged out of the door, keeping the wall on that side to his back, and crab walked his way down the hall, staying sighted on me until he reached the corner. Then he broke and ran.

I darted across the hall into the ballroom, and then had to hit the floor as a chair sailed over my head. The giant rat was using its tail to sweep furniture, or what was left of it, into the air at Greg. No wonder it sounded like they were still throwing tables. I snorted, because those pieces of furniture weren't going to be much of a deterrent for Greg, and I was right because Greg slammed into the thing. It gave a squeal as it tumbled backwards, hitting the floor hard enough to make it shake. Greg was on it, and the rat reared its head back, gnashing teeth, trying to find a grip on Greg's shoulder. Greg punched it. The back of its head hit the floor.

That thing had to have been tough because it shook the impact off, rolling and throwing Greg, who hit the floor and rolled. Its tail swept through the air to catch him in the chest as he was getting to his feet, and Greg slammed into a wall.

With him out of my range, the shadows and I raced forward. The thing caught sight of me and shrieked; I could see its eyes roll back, the whites showing. The figures ripped into it, long fingers carving furrows that soaked its fur in blood. It screamed and then charged me.

"Oh fuck!" I yelped. The figures billowed out again, the whispers howling, and it reared back, stumbling away from me. This time it ran from me, but instead of heading for the doors it went crashing through the windows at the back of the ballroom.

Greg had gotten free of the wall and chased after it, diving out the window without me.

Well damn it, now I'm going to have to go the long way around.

I started to head for the doors, but Virgil and Ranger came panting in before I had taken more than a few steps.

"What happened?" Virgil asked.

"Fuck," Ranger said. "Don't let him drive you anywhere."

Greg had come back in the window. "It got away."

"What got away?" Virgil snapped.

"The Rat King," I said. They stared at me. "What? It looks like a rat, and it had a horde of zombie rats. Ergo, Rat King."

"That's the best you could come up with?" Greg said, smiling at me.

"Am I right about it looking like a giant ass rat or not?"

"Yeah, it looked like a rat."

"And it had a horde of other, smaller, albeit zombie, rats."

"Is that what's left in the hall? Because that is insanely gross," Ranger said.

"Yes. I hope you didn't step in it, because Virgil's not going to want that in his car."

Both Virgil and Ranger checked their various boots.

"Who happened to the zombie rats?" Ranger asked.

"I did," I said. Virgil wouldn't have had to ask that question.

Ranger was giving me another one of those considering looks.

"So," I said, "are we settled on a name for it? Because I feel like Rat King is it."

Greg chuckled.

∞

After several minutes of arguing over who was driving back, which Virgil of course won, because it's his car, Ranger, Virgil and I headed back to the compound.

Greg had stayed behind to inform the police about what had happened, what to keep an eye out for, and to handle the reporters who had descended en masse to find out what was going on. Since he and Virgil were trying to limit my exposure to the press, probably so I wouldn't murder them for asking stupid questions, I got squished into the backseat.

I mean, Virgil offered me shotgun, but I didn't want Ranger sitting behind me. I wanted him in the front where I could keep an eye on him. Ranger, to his credit, had also said he wouldn't mind letting me sit up front, but I think that was because he was hoping to see less of Virgil's driving from the back.

When we got back, my knee popped as I was trying to climb out of the car, and when it does that, it's pretty loud. Ranger held out a hand. "Need some help?" he asked.

I finished climbing out. "No, I don't."

Ranger shrugged, dropped his hand. "Suit yourself."

"Pretty much," I said, steering around him. I went to follow Virgil across the garage and up the stairs.

Ranger fell into step next to me. "What happened to your knee?"

"It got dislocated." That was the extent of what Virgil would tell me about it. Which honestly made me glad I wasn't fully in my body when it happened because I'm not sure I want to know. The out of body experience might also be why I'm not having panic attacks over it more often. Easier to block it out if you can't remember most of it to begin with.

"War injury, huh?" Ranger asked.

"Maybe I'm just clumsy," I said.

Ranger stepped and turned so he was in front of me, blocking the path. I stopped, glaring up at him. Why do heroes always feel the need to get in my face? There was an expression on his face I wasn't quite sure how to read; his brow furrowed, a frown hovering at the corners of his mouth.

"Do you always deflect?" he asked me.

Not the question I was expecting. I paused, taking a moment to mull it over. "Not always," I finally said, wondering if honesty over sarcasm would get him to get out of my way for a change.

He looked surprised, and then he backed up. I skirted around him and headed up the stairs. He followed me. Virgil closed the bookcase in his room behind us.

"Meg," he said, "I'm staying up to let Greg in when he gets back. And I want to see if any of my contacts can put their ears to the ground about this Rat King of yours."

"He's not *my* Rat King," I muttered. I headed for my room, Ranger trailing behind me. When I headed in, Ranger paused, leaning against the doorframe. I shut the door in his face.

"Ow," he said, his voice muffled.

CHAPTER SIX

"Okay, Meg, we're going to take it from the top. Ranger, you set?" Virgil had positioned himself at the top of the steps.

"Yup," Ranger said, shaking out his hands. He was across the circle from me, well out of the ten-foot range.

I braced myself. The air around me twisted. My heartbeat pounded in my ears. The figures billowed forward, and everything around me sped back up.

"Again," Virgil called.

I clenched my teeth.

"I don't think doing this twenty more times is going to net us a different outcome," Ranger said. "She's breaking it every time."

Virgil was silent for a moment. "Meg, how long can you stand to stay in the effect?"

I glared at him. "I would prefer not to."

"For science," Virgil said.

I muttered to myself and pushed my hair back. Between the air gusting around me and the figures constantly swirling up, my hair was a tangled mess. I should've put it up. It was going to take me forever to get the knots out. I took a breath. "What did you want to try?" I asked.

"Ranger, I want you to try reversing her. What does she need to do?"

"She can just walk toward me. I'll only need a few steps."

"Meg?"

I scrubbed at my face. Greg's expression of irritation was rubbing off on me. "Fine. Jesus." It wasn't really fine to me. I could hear Greg grinding his teeth. "Stop that," I grumped.

"I didn't do anything yet," Ranger said.

"Not you," I said, irritated.

Greg cleared his throat.

Ranger was looking between the two of us, bemused.

"Are we done? Yes? Good. Meg, start walking. Don't break it this time," Virgil said.

I had taken about five steps toward Ranger before he hit me with his power. The air gusted around me, twisting; everything slowed, and then I could feel myself stepping backwards.

Being reversed is not any more of a comfortable experience than being slowed. It might actually be worse, and I had to fight not to let the figures out, because they didn't like that I didn't like it. I could hear the whispers calling for me to let them help.

Everything sped back up, and I was standing where I had started.

"Again," Virgil said.

"No," I snapped.

"Meg," Greg started, but I held up a hand.

"No. They want out. I need a break."

Virgil's phone rang, breaking the tension. He pulled it out but frowned when he saw who was calling. "What does she want?" he muttered, but he answered it anyway. "What do you want?"

I could see his eyes narrow. It was Virgil's don't fuck with me look, and it was generally as close to actually being angry as he got, which meant whoever was on the line with him was pissing him off. "Hold please," he said, his tone of voice surprisingly pleasant. He hit the mute button on the call and turned to me. "Susan would like a real interview with you."

"Hmm, no," I said.

"You may want to reconsider," Virgil said, "as she would like to interview you in exchange for not plastering the location of my compound all over the internet."

"Oh," I said. Someone had actually managed to get information they could blackmail Virgil with. My estimation of the reporter went up a notch. I still didn't like her, though; I was just impressed she would threaten Virgil in the first place. "I have conditions," I said.

"Indubitably," Virgil said. He unmuted. "She says yes. We'll discuss her conditions when you get here. Oh no, we're not coming to you, we're working. You'll have to come here," he listened for a moment. "Acceptable. Don't touch the gate." He hung up. "Meg, was that a long enough break, or do we need to take a lunch?"

I sighed. "How many more times?"

"You already know the answer to that. Now or later?"

"Give me a minute," I said. I called to the whispers, and they came, sighing in my ears. The figures swirled around me, and I reassured them. It would only be a little longer, and Ranger wasn't trying to hurt me. Could they wait for me to be done?

Yes, the whispers said, and I let them go.

"Okay," I said. "Ready." I stepped toward Ranger.

This time I could sense the whispers waiting, quiet in their sighs, the figures curling with them, patient in the ether.

Their serenity helped me stay calm. This was new. I made a mental note to talk to Virgil about it. I mean, there's a very good chance I'll conveniently forget to, since it would mean he would want to test more theories. But I still made the note.

Once Virgil was satisfied that not only could Ranger reverse me, but that I could also break that effect as well, he called a break for lunch. Then Greg's phone rang.

"Hello?" he said. A pause while he listened. "When?

Uh huh. You have the video from the first one too?" Another pause. "Yeah, I can head over now." Then he chuckled. "Yeah, I'll bring her with me."

Virgil, Ranger and I were all watching him.

"Well?" Virgil said.

"That was Detective White," Greg said. "She says another jewelry store got hit last night."

"And?"

"I'm getting to that," Greg said. "She wants Meg and me to come to the precinct to look at the videos from both."

"Why me?" I asked.

"She liked you," Greg said, grinning at me. "Said you were funny."

"Suit up," Virgil said, "and try to act like a professional."

"I'm professional," I protested. What? I can be.

Ranger was scowling at us. "Just you two, huh?"

"Just us two," Greg said. "That's all she requested."

∞

Police precincts make me nervous apparently. White was assigned to one of the larger ones, too, precinct four, a bustling place of beige walls and cracked linoleum. It was no nonsense, all business and full of cops. I don't have a problem with cops per se, I just tend to avoid being wherever they are. White had met us at the front desk as soon as the desk sergeant had let her know we were there. At least she didn't leave us cooling our heels. Maybe she's into professional courtesy.

"Fortress, Vengeance," she said, holding out a hand and shaking ours. Her grip was cool and firm. "Thank you for coming. This way please."

We followed her back down the hallway she had come from.

"What made you call us?" Greg asked.

"The situation is unusual," she said. "Here, I'll show you." She opened the door to an interview room. Inside was a small conference table, some chairs, and then a TV and video equipment on a cart. She waved at the chairs. "Have a seat."

Greg pulled out a chair for me and waited until I was seated. He sat in the one to my right so that my view of the TV would remain unobstructed.

Detective White fiddled with the TV and DVD player for a moment, then sat down on the table itself, her back to us. She pointed a remote, and the static disappeared, replaced with security footage from the first jewelry store.

The cases were being opened by rats. Greg and I both straightened up. "Are both the robberies like this?" Greg asked.

"Yes," she said. "And normally, I wouldn't have called you. But it's the second video that has me concerned." She got up and fiddled with the equipment again, replacing the DVD in the player with one that was sitting on top of it. Then she brought the new footage up. Again, more rats opening cases, pulling the jewelry out until something hulking moved into view of the camera. It was the Rat King from the charity event. It snarled, and ripped the camera down as the screen cut to static.

"The alarm didn't go off until that thing went into the store itself," she said. "I don't know if he got impatient or what, but I'm not equipped to deal with, well, whatever that thing is."

"Rat King," I said.

"Hmm," she said. "Rat King. Fitting. I brought this to my captain's attention, because fuck if I'm going to risk anyone on my team going after him. I do robbery, not monsters."

"Villain," I said absently. "Colloquial term is villain, although he appears - what is that, mutated? Spliced?"

"Those aren't a thing, that's comic books. Maybe a shifter type," Greg said, still studying the screen.

"Semantics," she said. "Doesn't matter what he is."

Greg had leaned around me, one arm resting on the table, his chest pressed against my shoulder and the back of my chair. "What do you need from us? Retrieval?"

"I'm sure the insurance companies would appreciate

that. If you can, figure out where the thi – Rat King, is hiding," she said. "In the meantime, if any more robberies happen that involve him or his cohorts, I'll give you a call." Well, that was a dismissal if I've ever heard one.

We stood and left the interview room. Another detective passed by us in the hall: suit pants, tie, button down shirt, thinning brown hair, build thickening around the middle.

"Fucking heroes," he muttered once he was behind us. My hearing might not be as good as Greg's, but his mutter had that volume to it where you knew he meant for us to hear it.

"Mason," Greg said. His hand was on the small of my back, gently urging me to continue.

"Heard me, did you?" Mason said, still behind us, but now he was following.

"You know I did," Greg said calmly.

"Whose case you here to stick your nose in now?" Mason asked. He had caught up to and come around in front of us, forcing Greg and I to stop or shove him out of our way. The way Greg moved was so subtle I didn't realize he did it until he had placed himself in front of me, forcing Mason to back up a step or get knocked down.

"We're here by department request," Greg said. "If you don't like it, take it up with your captain."

Mason didn't answer him at first, then he took the opportunity to lean to the side, eyeing me. "Who're you? I didn't realize *Fortress* took on trainees," he sneered.

I stared him down. "You sure you want to know?" Because the whispers were tugging at me.

Greg half turned so he could look at me and catch my eyes. "Vengeance," he said.

"Jesus," Mason said. "Are all of you so fucking dramatic?"

"Oh no, they were having a special on drama when they made me, so I got double," I said.

Mason grunted; he sounded surprised. "She's funny. You should keep her around."

"I'll do that," Greg said. Mason moved around us and continued back down the hallway in the direction he had been headed before he felt the need to confront us.

"He always that friendly?" I asked Greg.

"He was downright pleasant today," he said. We had headed out the front doors, into the sun where Greg scooped me up and took off.

∞

Once we were back at the compound, I had to do something about my hair. Between Virgil's testing of the various immunities Ranger and I had to each other and then Greg flying me back and forth from the city, it was one giant rat's nest. Ha, get it? Fine, don't laugh. I thought it was a great pun.

I didn't want to take a full-on shower because it was going to take me too long to get everything untangled, and Virgil isn't exactly set up on city water. I didn't need to be running the well dry. I set my things up on the side of the tub, settled a towel over my shoulders, and stuck my head under the faucet.

It had been over thirty minutes when Greg knocked on the door and poked his head in. I'm surprised he gave me that long based on the amount of swearing I was doing. "Do you want some help?" he asked.

"These fucking knots," I said. I was trying to finger detangle them, because I didn't want to rip my hair out with the comb. "I should just cut it off."

"You don't want to do that," he said, half soothing, half amused.

"I thought you were supposed to be helping," I said.

He huffed, came over and knelt next to me by the tub. "Where's the conditioner?"

I twisted my head to look at him. "Do I look like I can point it out to you right now?" My fingers were stuck, and I was trying to pull them out without causing breakage or ripping my hair out by the roots.

Look, I take a lot of pride in my hair, regardless of the fact that I shove it back into a ponytail a lot. Other than my winning personality, it's my best feature.

Greg grinned at me. "No, you don't look like you can do much of anything right now." He leaned forward, his lips hovering over mine, as he shifted so that I was trapped against the tub with him behind me.

"Don't you dare," I said.

His fingers grazed up my sides, and I shrieked, trying to squirm away, yanking my fingers out of my curls and then, just to get back at him for tickling me, I flung my wet hair back in his face. He yanked his head out of the way, his fingers back at my side, one hand slipping along my stomach, his other on my ribs, skimming along.

I laughed, and bucked back against him, still trying to wriggle out of his grasp. He had one arm up, wrapped across my front, hand on my shoulder, pinning me to his chest. His other came to rest on my hip. I had twisted my head to look at him, and my hair was dripping water everywhere, over his shoulder and shirt, down the towel that was half slipped off my back. His lips were hovering over mine again.

"Meg," he said. I kissed him. Because I knew that tone of voice he was using, and I wasn't ready for what he wanted to tell me yet. He pulled back, his hand coming off my shoulder to rest against my face, his thumb brushing my cheek.

"Are you done in there yet?" Ranger said from the door.

Greg's fingers flexed against my hip, even as he dropped his hand from my face. A flash of disappointment mixed in with the annoyance on his face.

"No," I said. "I'm not done."

"There's only the one bathroom," Ranger said.

"Sucks to be you," I said. Greg had loosened his arm, so I leaned back over the tub, gathering up my hair and shaking it out upside down. Water went splattering across the bottom. I reached for the conditioner, but Greg had already grabbed it, his other hand on my elbow.

"Come on, kitchen sink," he said.

"I'm comfortable here," I said.

"Meg," he said, irritation in his voice. I twisted my head to look at him, eyes narrowed, because he better not be irritated at me. I could see the entreaty in his eyes.

"Fine," I huffed. I yanked the towel back off my shoulders to contain my hair so I wasn't dripping water all the way down to the kitchen. I got up and shoved my way past Ranger, leaving Greg to gather up my hair care paraphernalia.

I was already leaning over the sink, running fresh water through my curls by the time Greg caught up to me. He set everything down on the counter next to me. I turned off the water, but he had already squirted conditioner into his palms, and set to work on getting it into my hair, his fingers massaging at the scalp.

"Mmmm," I said, closing my eyes. He leaned over and kissed my neck, his hands stilling. "Excuse me, tangles," I said.

He chuckled, and went back to my hair, making short work of the knots that were still there. The man has magic fingers. In more ways than one. Yeah, I said it. Shut up.

Once he had the knots out, I snagged the comb. Look, you want me to explain this whole routine to you? Because you're going to need to take notes. There's a lot of info.

Greg leaned against the cabinets, resting one arm on the counter. "Meg," he started again, but he stopped, and his head turned toward the kitchen door as Ranger came striding in.

"You're still doing your hair?" Ranger asked.

"If someone hadn't interrupted me, I'd already be done," I said. It was meant to be aimed at Ranger for kicking us out of the bathroom in the first place.

"Maybe attack dog should let you have some alone time," Ranger said, as he went into the fridge.

It's really hard to glare at someone when your head is upside down.

Greg had plucked the comb from my hands and was gently pulling it through my hair, one hand resting on my hip because he had placed himself between Ranger and me.

"What, can't let her do things for herself?" Ranger asked, having straightened up from the fridge.

Greg's fingers flexed against me again, and he stepped closer to me, so that his hips brushed against mine. He was leaning just over my back, on the pretext of checking my hair for more knots, but I knew what he was really doing.

"I think you're good now," he said. He took a step back to my other side, one hand still resting on my hip.

"Thanks," I said, and then shot another glare at Ranger. "Is the bathroom free now, or is someone going to have another *emergency*?"

"Oh, don't let me stop you," Ranger said, leaning against the fridge.

"Do you actually need something or are you blocking the fridge for no reason?" Greg asked.

"That depends on who needs to get in it." Ranger crossed his arms. "Since we're guarding people, places and things."

"What exactly are you implying?" Greg asked, his tone cool.

"I'm not implying anything. Not my problem if you can't read between the lines. Although can you read?"

I was done with the posturing. I'm not a fucking prize, and while Greg would get an earful from me later, Ranger wasn't getting away with making a snide comment like that. I flipped my hair, water-laden conditioner splattering against Ranger's jacket and the fridge. Damn it, I missed. Virgil was going to make me wipe the fridge off, and now I had water dripping down my back and shirt.

Greg's lips twitched. Behind me I could hear Ranger brushing the water off the leather of his jacket.

"Oops," I mouthed at Greg. He broke into a grin.

"Incorrigible," he said, but he wrapped an arm around

my waist, and kissed the side of my forehead, despite the water dripping down my face now.

"I'm going to go rinse my hair out," I said. That was a lie, there's more to do. But I'm not taking the time to explain it to you.

"Hmm," Greg said.

I headed for the kitchen door, just as Virgil came in. He stopped, taking in the tableau. "Why are you washing your hair in my kitchen?"

"Someone needed the bathroom," I said, marching by him.

CHAPTER SEVEN

Susan was early.

Virgil opened up the gate for her, and we all went out to meet her, Ranger included. Virgil had set up those folding tailgate chairs outside for us. Based on the way my power tended to respond to my emotions, Virgil didn't want his furniture getting shredded if Susan mis-stepped. Plus, he could get her out of my range if necessary.

Virgil was the one who went down from the steps to greet her; Ranger and Greg moved forward while I hung behind, the most physically vulnerable member kept at the back.

It was irksome.

"You're early," Virgil grunted to Susan by way of greeting.

"My mother always said if you're on time, you're late," Susan said with a smile, ignoring Virgil's mood. "Ranger, nice to see you again. Looks like Vengeance had the time to show you the sights after all?" I didn't like the implication in her tone.

Greg tensed.

Ranger crossed his arms. "Oh no, I'm here for business."

Susan's smile didn't falter. "Hmm. What kind of business?"

"Can't say, need to know only," Ranger said.

Well, this was interesting. Was Ranger going to present a united front? Susan was silent for a moment before addressing me. "Are we ready? I have questions prepared so we can go in—"

"No," Virgil said. "We're sitting outside. I'm not letting you in my house."

Susan smirked. "Bit paranoid, aren't you?"

Virgil pointed. "Sit. And Vengeance has conditions."

"Of course," Susan chose a chair and the rest of us moved to take seats. Greg hovered by my elbow until I was seated. There were no jockeying or remarks from Ranger now, like he had been making in the kitchen and living room during breaks and meals. Virgil seated himself last, adjusting his chair so that he could see us all without having to turn his head.

Susan watched us. "You know, I don't think we need a full entourage. It's just an interview."

I sighed. "It's easier just to ignore them."

Susan had her recorder and a pad of paper and pen out. "Do they not trust you?"

Virgil answered. "No, it's that we don't trust you."

"You let me go off with her alone once before."

"Hmm, that was before you threatened me," Virgil said. "Now you're a problem, and I don't like problems."

Susan watched him coolly. Everyone was silent. It was making me itch, but Greg had set a hand on mine, and given me a small headshake, so I bit down on the comments I wanted to make.

"You said there are conditions?" Susan finally said.

"No questions related to Vengeance's parents," said Virgil, "and her relationship with Fortress stays off the record."

Susan narrowed her eyes. "Fine, I can work with that," she turned slightly in her chair, leaning on the arm so she was facing me. "So, Vengeance, why now?"

"Why now what?" I asked.

She simply breezed by my attitude, "Why hero work

now? Why didn't you join up sooner?"

"Hadn't been recruited by the right person. I don't play well with others."

"Was Fortress the one who recruited you?"

"Nope," I said. I mean, Greg had tried for about two seconds. But he hadn't been the one to convince me.

"So, Vigilante recruited you? I thought he worked alone."

"I also don't play well with others, so our styles mesh," Virgil told her. "And Vengeance has been doing hero work without garnering attention for years. It's how I knew we would work well together." Well, that was the first inkling I had gotten that Virgil had been keeping an eye on me. I suppose I shouldn't be surprised.

Susan looked back at me. "Why didn't you want the attention? Most heroes seem to enjoy the glamour."

"Because I didn't want the attention."

"There has to be—"

"No," I said. "No, there doesn't have to be more to it. I just didn't want it." I had wanted quiet, normal.

Susan pursed her lips. "I understand you've displayed this ability since you were small?"

"Don't most of us?" I asked.

"Well, yes, but your—" she paused, "my sources say that even as a baby there were . . . incidents."

"Well considering I wouldn't remember any of that, I don't have an answer for you."

"They never—" and she was skirting too close.

"No, *they*, never," I snarled. I could feel the press of the whispers, fingers on my neck. Next to me, Greg shuddered. I let them go. Virgil and Ranger had tensed, and there was no way Susan had missed the unease in the air, but she cleared her throat.

I had seen the way Ranger's eyes had flicked to my neck while the figures were there. Sometimes the way the figures curl those fingers of theirs they encircle my throat, a necklace of bleeding ink and drifting smoke. I could see the question in his face. Was my power ever a threat to me? They weren't, but I wasn't going to explain them to him. I was theirs and they were mine.

"What, exactly, is your power?" she asked. "I saw the bank footage. How did you get them to turn on each other like that?"

I didn't know how I wanted to answer that. The question wasn't unexpected, I just didn't know how much truth to give her. "I turned their fear back on them," I said, settling for the lie.

"So, you make people afraid? That seems – like a soft power."

"I think the results speak for themselves," I said.

She clicked her tongue. Leaned forward in her chair. "From what my sources have told me, you're not telling me the truth."

"Maybe your sources are liars."

She gave me a long, thoughtful look. "My sources said they would like to meet with you."

"No," I said. "I'm not interested in meeting with your sources. We're done here." I hopped off my chair and went inside, leaving Susan outside with the men. I could hear Greg interrupt her protests, and then I was going down the stairs, the walls of the safe house cutting off outside sounds.

I headed for the kitchen, pulled a soda out of the fridge. Virgil only stocks them because I want them. Other than that, he's as bad as Greg is about the no sugar in the house thing. If it doesn't come from fruit or honey, they won't eat it. Well, that and the occasional latte that Greg will get.

Weirdos.

I popped the top on the soda, leaning on the island, watching the door while I waited.

Footsteps sounded down the hall. Boots, which meant not Greg.

Ranger appeared in the doorway, and he leaned against

the frame, arms crossed. He watched me.

I was getting really tired of people staring at me. "What?" I snapped.

"You always end conversations like that?" he asked.

"Like what?"

"That thing you do, where you storm off."

"Depends on how badly you piss me off," I said. Because sometimes I just terrify them into leaving me alone.

He came off the doorframe, around the island, brushing against me to get in the fridge. He pulled a soda out.

"Those are mine," I said.

"Mhmm," he said, opening it and taking a sip as he backed up to the other side of the island. "What're you gonna do about it?" He winked at me. The figures swirled, and one of them reached out and knocked the can out of his hand. It hit the floor, soda spraying, and then they were gone. Ranger looked down at his now wet boots, shaking soda off his hand. "Wow. Petty."

I smirked at him. "You'll learn that about me." I took a sip of my soda.

"You gonna clean that up?"

"I'm not the one who dropped my soda."

His lips twitched, and I could see a gleam of amusement in his eyes. Guess I was going to have to work harder to make him mad instead of interested.

Virgil came in. Saw the soda on the floor. "Meg."

"Wasn't me. Ranger dropped his."

"Always with you and the bus," Ranger said, but he was grabbing the can off the floor. "Where are the paper towels?"

"Under the sink," Virgil said.

"These are towel towels."

"Yup," I said. "Virgil and Greg don't believe in trashing Mother Earth." They honestly had a lot in common, which explained why they had become friends in the first place.

"You still have to use water to wash these," Ranger said, wiping soda off the floor and the side of the island cabinets.

"Where do you want these?"

"Laundry room is in the garage," Virgil said. He was busy looking through the fridge.

"Where exactly in the garage?"

Virgil sighed. "Meg, would you show him? I know exactly how that soda ended up on the floor."

I rolled my eyes. "Fine." I left my soda on the counter. Out the kitchen, through Virgil's room, down the stairs, Ranger trailed behind me. Straight across the garage to the other side, I pointed out the door clearly marked, *Laundry*. "There you go." I turned to head back, but he grabbed my arm when I tried to step past him. I scowled.

"Don't let the reporters get to you," he said. "They're just doing their jobs."

"Oh, you mean sticking their noses in my business? No thank you."

He chuckled. "Being nosy is their job. You'll get used to the answering without actually answering before you know it." He let go of my arm and continued to the laundry room. I retreated up the stairs back to the kitchen.

∞

"Patrols, let's go." Virgil came sailing into the living room, where Greg and I were seated. Well, Ranger was there too, on the other side of the room. He had been looking through the books on the shelves and occasionally stepping in front of the TV while he wandered back and forth. I think he was trying to irritate Greg because Greg had chosen the show we were watching. But the only person he was managing to irritate was me, because Greg had only picked it because he knew I liked it.

It's *Adventure Time* since you have to know so badly. Greg hates it.

Okay, Greg might be irritated because I was getting irritated. I could feel it from the way his arm tensed against me, and his fingers kept flexing.

Yes, Virgil replaced the damn TV. He did not make me pay for it.

"Is that a good idea?" Greg asked. "That thing is still out there; I don't think we should be sending Meg on her own."

Ranger snorted.

"You got an opinion?" Greg asked. I could hear the warning in Greg's tone, that he didn't really care what Ranger's opinion was, unless it was one he didn't like.

"Yeah, I do," Ranger said.

"You going to share with the class?" Greg asked.

"No, I don't think I will," Ranger said. "Meg's the one who has to put up with you being controlling."

That sounded like sharing an opinion with the class to me. The awkward silence stretched, but Greg and I both seemed to be reluctant to break it with protestations, because we both knew he was struggling to let me out of his sight and into danger. Even Virgil seemed at a loss for words as to how to salvage the current mood we had just been tossed into.

Probably because he kind of sort of agreed with Ranger.

"Greg, you're in the air. Meg, Ranger, you're in the Hummer with me. No foot patrols," Virgil finally said, conceding to Greg as best he could.

Greg heaved himself off the couch, turning to offer me a hand up, and I took it. He didn't let go once I was up though; we simply followed Virgil hand in hand down to the garage. He was marking his territory again, and eventually I was going to need to put my foot down. Ranger trailed behind us.

The doors to the Hummer swung open before we reached them. Virgil waved a hand at the tunnel for the garage ramp. "Go. We'll catch up to you."

Greg bent and caught my lips with his before he stepped back. "Watch yourself," he said.

"I'll stick close," I promised him. He took off, the boom of his passage echoing off the tunnel walls once he hit the main entrance.

"I wish he wouldn't do that," Virgil grumbled, but he hauled himself up into the driver's seat, and I climbed in behind him, snagging the Kevlar off the floor where I had left it from the docks.

No, I had not been wearing it when we first encountered Rat King. We had all rushed out of there too quickly.

Ranger got into the back seat on the passenger side. I side eyed him over the metal hump separating us. "You don't want to ride up front?"

"No. I've seen—" Ranger didn't finish his sentence because Virgil had hit the gas, and the Hummer was roaring forward. "Motherfucker." He grabbed wildly, one hand set on the door.

A lighter vehicle would have come jumping off the ramp. Fortunately, Virgil had the gate open already, so I didn't have to watch him dodge it. The Hummer is a big vehicle; it's not going to have the maneuverability of the Cobra.

We spent the rest of the drive to Malus City in silence. Which for me, once I had that outfit on over my clothes and had stopped moving around, was ridiculously hard. Yeah, don't tell Greg I wasn't buckled in while I was getting that stupid thing on.

Once we hit the city streets and were crisscrossing our way back and forth, Virgil hit the police scanner. I say scanner, but it's legitimate law enforcement equipment, the same radio you would find in any officer's vehicle.

Look, Virgil has everything. When he says friends in high places, he means he has friends in all places, including the low ones. Pretty sure some of the stuff he has wasn't acquired legally. Virgil operates in a very grey area.

Ranger was leaning forward, elbows on knees. "What're we looking for?"

"Anything," Virgil said. "Muggings, break ins, assault. Watch the streets. I'm not picky about what kind of crime we stop."

"That's a breath of fresh air," Ranger said.

"What's a breath of fresh air?" I asked, not entirely sure if I was curious or irritated and looking for an argument. Possibly both.

Ranger snorted. "Most heroes don't consider it worth their time if they're not going to end up on the evening news."

Huh. Well, that had definitely been my overall opinion of heroes, so I guess Ranger found something we both agree on. I didn't tell him that though.

"What type of hero is attack dog?" Ranger asked. "He strikes me as the 'only if its newsworthy' type."

"He has a name," I said.

"So, newsworthy type."

I shot him a glare.

"I'm not hearing a no," Ranger said, "so that must be a yes."

"Greg is more the 'no civilian casualties' type," Virgil said.

"Isn't that all heroes?" I asked.

"It should be," Ranger muttered.

"Accidents happen," Virgil said. "Greg doesn't accept those as a matter of course."

Well, that wasn't really news to me with the way he had refused to let me be used as bait for a villain of epic proportions, even though that would've made his life a whole lot easier at the time. You know, without the whole dramatic hauling off of me, running to Virgil in the first-place escapade.

And I certainly didn't make it easy on him not to let me get killed in the first place.

The radio crackled to life. "10-57, corner of 51st and Broad—"

"We checking that one out?" Ranger asked, but Virgil had already swung the Hummer into the next right.

"It's probably nothing," Virgil said, "but yes."

The maneuverability of the Hummer doesn't matter much when the driver can just shove cars out of his way. Virgil had gassed it, the vehicle barreling down the streets, the rumble of the tires as he took corners because the Hummer does not squeal. It thunders.

By the time we reached the spot for the firearm discharge call, a squad car was already there. The police were talking to a couple of people, who were motioning at the sidewalk further up. Virgil slowed and stopped the Hummer.

"Hmm," he said.

"Meg, go talk to them," Ranger said.

"Why me?" I asked.

"Because you're cute. Flirt a little. They'll eat it up."

"I don't do flirting," I said.

"You," Ranger said, and he stopped, the look on his face bemused. "What do you mean you don't flirt?" he finally demanded. "Who doesn't flirt?"

"Meg doesn't flirt," Virgil said from up front.

"Then what—" Ranger started again. "You know what, never mind. What do you do to get answers?"

"I scare them into telling me," I said.

"I'm sorry, is that what counts for acceptable procedure here?"

Virgil shrugged. "It does when Meg's involved."

"How do you reconcile that?" Ranger demanded. "You can't go making people rip themselves apart to get answers, that's—"

"Villain shit?" I asked archly, "I don't go that hard with people who haven't done anything wrong." I was pulling off the seatbelt, a hand on the door handle.

"Whoa, whoa, no. You're not going. I'll talk to them," Ranger said.

"Meg, go with him," Virgil said.

"Not if she's gonna do the freaky demon shit with the cops," Ranger said.

I rolled my eyes. "By the time you finish arguing over who's going, the cops and the bad guy will be long gone."

"No demon shit," Ranger said.

"Jesus, fine," I said. I hopped out, and Ranger had to

scramble to catch up to me from his side of the car because I was already crossing the street.

"God damn it, wait!" he said.

"Be faster next time," I told him.

The cops had spotted us, and they squared off; one had his arms crossed, one had his hands on hips, fingers hovering by his firearm.

"We come in peace," Ranger said, hands slightly up, palms out. "What happened?"

"Nothing we can't handle," the one with crossed arms said. "We've already got a report."

Ranger mirrored his stance. "Yeah? Which way did he go?"

One of the people, a teen in a green shirt and jeans on the sidewalk pointed down to our left. "That way."

Ranger smirked at the cops who were scowling at us. "Got a description?" he asked.

"About five ten, brown hair, brown hoodie, jeans, white sneakers," said the helpful teenager. "He was waving a gun around and then shot the tree."

"Thanks," Ranger said, turning toward me. "Wanna take a walk?"

"I don't think—"

Virgil hit the horn and waved at us. "Go, I'll circle the block," he called over.

How the fuck did he hear us?

Ranger held out his arm, an invitation to proceed with him.

I rolled my eyes and started up the sidewalk, and he fell into step beside me. "That didn't look like flirting to me," I said.

"They're not going to think I'm cute," he said. "I was at a disadvantage there."

"You don't know which way they swing," I said. "Kind of close minded of you."

"Not because of that," Ranger said. "Because they're

cops. I don't look defenseless. I look like a threat, at least to them. But you, you walk up all fragile-looking, acting like a concerned citizen, they'll bend over backwards for you."

I was silent.

"What? No comeback for that?" Ranger asked.

"I don't play those kinds of games," I said.

"Why not? You don't take advantage of the gifts God gave you?"

"I'm not sure He had much to do with it."

"Yeah, yours might come from the other place," Ranger said. "So, I don't know why you put up with attack dog."

I stopped, swinging to face him. "I don't see how that has anything to do with it."

"Yeah? You okay with him telling you what to do?"

I snorted. "Nobody tells me what to do." I started walking again, my steps speeding up with the intention of outpacing Ranger.

He had longer legs than me, though, and he had no trouble keeping up with me. I would have to run if I wanted to out distance him. "He doesn't?" Ranger continued. "Because from what I remember at the fire, he told you to stay somewhere specific and then was pissed when you didn't."

"I don't recall you being present for that conversation," I said.

"I can read between the lines when it comes to someone saying that's not where I left you."

I stopped again. "That—" I started, but I wasn't sure why I was defending my or Greg's choices or words to him. I didn't need approval from someone who had a quarter of the picture. "You know what, I'm done here."

"Why? Because I'm right?" he asked, chasing after me as I started up the sidewalk again.

"No, because you're way off base, and I'm not going to stand here and defend my relationship to you."

"Your supposedly solid relationship?" he said. "The one where I don't stand a chance?"

"Yes, that one, and you don't," I said, stopping again because I'm an idiot and can't not argue.

"Then what was the thing with the soda?" he demanded, stepping into my space. "You say you don't flirt; you can't tell me that wasn't flirting."

I was left momentarily speechless. Had I been encouraging him without realizing it? When what I was trying to do was get him to back off and leave me alone?

Had Greg noticed and that was why he was being so territorial right now? Oh, he was going to get an earful if he had noticed that and hadn't just asked me about what was going on. I would've modified my behavior to full on retreat mode. Can't misread someone for flirting with you if they won't talk to you at all in the first place.

I took a step back from him. I needed space, and he was still watching me, waiting for an answer. And I didn't know what to say. I wasn't sure he would believe a denial.

Movement to my right up the sidewalk caught my eye, and we both turned to look. Brown hoodie, jeans, white sneakers. Ranger took off, and I followed after him, because I'm not staying behind on a random sidewalk.

"Hey! Wait up!" Ranger yelled. Brown Hoodie glanced over his shoulder; apparently he didn't like what he saw and sped up. We sped up too, and then Brown Hoodie put his head down and started sprinting.

"For the – God damn it, I hate it when they run," Ranger said, but he broke into a run as well. I followed, calling on the whispers.

I was faster. "On your left," I said, dodging around Ranger, the whispers, figures, shadows and I flowing together.

"What-?" he was trying and failing to keep up with me. "Slow down, damn it! We shouldn't get separated!"

I ignored him. The whispers and I were gaining on Brown Hoodie, and he made the mistake of looking back to see where we were. The figures slammed into him because he had to slow, and they knocked him to the ground. He screamed, surprise and fear, the figures and shadows billowing over and around him. He had his arms up, trying to cover his face and head.

"Vengeance! Stop, damn it!" Ranger almost slammed into me. I felt the moment at my back where he had to jerk himself away before he knocked me down when he came to his own sudden stop.

But the figures and shadows were retreating, circling, eddying around me. Ranger stepped around me and up to Brown Hoodie.

"I want to talk to you," he told the guy on the ground.

"Fuck off, man!" he yelled. His hands were scrabbling, trying to yank something out of his jacket pocket, and Ranger kicked him. Brown Hoodie yelped as a gun clattered to the ground. He tried to roll and lunge for it, but Ranger kicked him again and then set his boot on the guy's chest when he rolled back to try and get out of the way of Ranger's feet.

"You want to talk now?" Ranger asked.

"I know my rights!"

"I'm not a cop," Ranger said, "so I don't give a shit about your rights. Why were you waving a gun around and committing arborcide?"

"I didn't shoot nobody!"

"The tree dumbass. Why'd you shoot the tree?"

"Man, I didn't shoot shit."

"Then why'd you run?"

"You'd run too if you saw her behind you. Damn. You don't watch the news?"

Ranger looked over at me. "You believe him?"

I crossed my arms. "Do you?"

"Do you ever just answer the question?"

"No," I said.

Ranger smirked at me. "No, huh?" I wasn't sure we were still on the topic of the guy on the ground anymore.

"No," I repeated.

"Look, man, if you're not gonna come to a conclusion

sometime soon I got things to do," Brown Hoodie said.

Ranger pulled his boot off the man's chest and set it over top of the gun. "You can go, but I'm keeping this."

"Excuse me?" I said.

"Can you prove it's the guy?" Ranger asked. But it wouldn't have mattered if I could because he hadn't waited for anything more and had already gotten to his feet, a gust of wind as he rose and then he had taken off. The guy was gone, and I wasn't sure what Ranger's game had been.

"I thought we were supposed to catch the bad guys," I said.

"And we caught someone."

"You let him go," I said.

"Yeah, because he says he didn't do it, and all we've got is circumstantial evidence." He bent down and picked up the gun. "Well, now we have evidence – provided the cops do their job. Once they dig the bullet out of that tree, they can match it to the gun that did it."

"I don't see how that helps since you let the guy go."

"Oh, ye of little faith," Ranger said, waggling a wallet at me. "I have his ID."

I scowled because I didn't want to admit I was impressed at the forethought.

The Hummer rumbled up to the curb. Virgil had come around to us, and the doors swung open. "Anything?" he asked.

"Yeah," Ranger said. "We got some stuff to drop off at the station. Who's in charge of this shit over there?"

CHAPTER EIGHT

At the front desk, Ranger set the gun and the wallet down on the counter. The desk sergeant stared at him for a moment.

"What's this?" he finally grunted.

"Concerned citizen, dropping off items someone dropped on the sidewalk," Ranger said. "Corner of Fifty-First and Broad. Think you've got a report for an incident over there earlier tonight."

The desk sergeant eyed us again for a moment before scooping the items off the counter and stowing them back behind it. He was scribbling something down. "Did you see who dropped it?"

"Yeah, about five ten, brown hair, brown hoodie, jeans, white sneakers. Broke and ran when we tried to tell him he dropped something."

"Iver, you letting the riffraff in again?" a voice called. He strode up to the counter, leaning on it with one arm, giving Ranger the same squint-eyed stare he had given Greg. He turned his attention over to Virgil and me, standing just a few feet behind.

"Vengeance," Mason said. "The dramatic one. Where's Fortress? He lose you?"

"He hasn't yet," I said. "I'm pretty hard to shake off."

He actually laughed. He must be in a pleasant mood again. "What brings you to the station?"

"Concerned citizen shit."

Mason bared his teeth. "What, with these two jokers? You're better than that."

"Better than what?" I asked.

"I heard about that interview with Susan," Mason said, ignoring my question and switching topics. "I've never seen a reporter so pissed not to have a live, on camera interview. All she had was that little recorder to play. I especially liked the part where you told her you were done here."

"I didn't realize she was sharing that around," Virgil said.

"She was over here trying to convince some of us to ferret out more info. The whole 'you scratch my back, I'll scratch yours' spiel."

Beside me, Virgil shifted. "Ferret out what info?" His tone had sharpened.

Mason shrugged. "She thinks there's more to the whole Vengeance story than what she's getting. Heard through the grapevine that interview with her parents was pretty disappointing," he turned back toward me. "Keep on not giving her shit. I like that about you."

"Thought it was my dramatics you liked."

"Those too," he said. "You seem alright for a hero."

"I'm not really the heroing type," I said.

"Must be why then," Mason knocked his knuckles against the counter. "That why you here with, whatever these two clowns are supposed to be?"

I looked at Ranger and Virgil, trying to figure out what he was talking about. Ranger was in his usual leather jacket, the reinforced motorcycle pants, you know, biker stuff. It looks kind of like tactical armor to me. Don't know if the steel-toed boots matched the rest of the look he was going for.

Virgil was in a duster, paratrooper style cargo pants, and combat boots. He looks like some sort of *Blade* knock-off wannabe. The fact that his pants are tucked into his boots doesn't help.

Both of them were in all black, and here I was in basically a suit of Kevlar, also in all black. This thing is bulky, and basically shaped like a set of bulletproof overalls. But with sleeves.

Virgil kind of went all out with the "make sure Meg doesn't get shot" armor.

I mean, yeah, I guess they kind of gave off a "We take ourselves very, very seriously but dress like a couple of idiots" kind of vibe? But I'm pretty sure all three of us looked silly.

"And what are you wearing?" Mason asked, having continued while I was studying Virgil and Ranger.

"Kevlar?" I asked, with that "isn't it obvious?" sort of tone to my voice.

"Why? Don't you all have, I don't know, resilience?"

"I don't want to get shot," I said, choosing to gloss by the fact that I don't have any of the extra hardiness part. "I heard it hurts."

Mason's lips twitched. "It's not that bad," he said.

"Still don't want to find out."

He grunted. He hadn't moved off the desk yet, and I was trying to figure out why he was still standing around talking to us. I had gotten the impression that he had a bone to pick with heroes, so I wasn't sure why he was so interested in me.

"When Susan was here who did she talk to?" Virgil asked, switching back to the earlier topic.

Mason stood there, scratched his cheek. He stared Virgil down without answering him. The silence stretched while he seemed to be weighing something. "You were on that recording too," he said finally.

"Hmm," Virgil said. "I was running interference."

Mason scoffed. "Interference for what?"

"My dramatics," I said.

I surprised another laugh out of him. "Iver, you ever see a hero with a sense of humor before?" he asked.

"Nope," Iver said.

"First time for everything," Mason said. He knocked his knuckles on the desk again. "Where's that appointment sheet?"

"Susan didn't have any appointments," Iver said, handing up a clipboard.

Mason flipped through the sheets, pausing on a page and running a finger down it. "No, no she didn't. Hmm, let's see, she talked to me, where I told her I didn't have any info for her, White, who also told her she had no info. She talk to you Iver?"

"I'm just a desk sergeant. I wouldn't have anything to tell her anyway."

Mason chuckled. "I love when reporters think they're better than us. Let's see, Johnson, Delle, and Howell. Just those last three that I'm aware of." He handed the clipboard back to Iver.

Virgil had his hand up at his chin. "Why those three?"

Mason shrugged. "Johnson's the one who usually deals with you assholes. He's the - what's the word? - liaison."

"Delle and Howell?"

Mason was silent again, mouth set, staring Virgil down. Virgil was watching him.

"I see," Virgil said. "Talkative types, huh?"

Mason seemed to relax. "They're social-like," he admitted.

"How social?" Virgil asked.

"Why does it matter?" I asked. "I haven't met any of those others. What are they going to say? Yup, saw her on the news?"

"Very social," Mason said, sailing by my interjection. "You watch out for those two if you don't want the extra attention. They like being in the limelight, even if it's only by association."

Ranger was also leaning on the desk counter, mimicking Mason's stance. He kept doing that around people, and I wasn't sure if he did it on purpose to mock them or if it was unconscious, a chameleon effect.

"You're not a limelight kind of person?" he asked Mason.

Mason shot him a look. "No. Unlike you, I have real work to do. Murder cases don't solve themselves."

"I thought you were robbery," Virgil said.

Mason grunted. "Transferred departments. Homicide was shorthanded. Lot of cases going on the back burner because we didn't have the manpower," he said, then glared over at Ranger. "Lots of city funds going toward enticing heroes to move here for the glamour when there are better uses for that money."

"Oh, I get it. Because I'm new here," Ranger said. "I didn't get one of those special invitations. I'm just a tourist."

Hmm, so Ranger wasn't planning on staying. Good, I didn't need him sticking around, tricking me into flirting with him.

Shut up, that wasn't my intention, and you know it.

Mason seemed to be on the same page as me. "Good," he grunted. "We've got too many attention whores in this city as it is." His eyes flicked over to me. "Excuse the language."

"No, I think Vengeance likes it when people tell it like it is," Ranger said. "Clear communication is key with her, apparently."

I scowled at him. "I don't have time for other people's shit. Especially when they misread the situation."

"I think I'm reading the situation just fine," Ranger said. "The situation is that – what's your name?" he asked, turning to Mason.

"Mason."

"The situation is that Mason here doesn't like heroes because we're all a bunch of attention-seekers and don't do any of the real work. I get that right?"

Mason grunted again.

"That sounds about right to me," Iver said from behind the desk.

"Great," I said. "Glad we got that cleared up. Because I

was totally lost."

Mason and Iver snorted.

"Hmm," Virgil said, taking the diplomatic route of not pointing out my sarcasm. "We should be going. I believe we've fulfilled our civic duty by handing over those items for lost and found."

We turned and headed out the doors, leaving Mason and Iver watching us from the desk.

∞

One of Virgil's contacts finally got back to him. The most he could tell him was that the Rat King wasn't from around here. Virgil was reaching out across the pond to see what he could find out from foreign contacts. Not just reports of a giant rat, but odd thefts, any video footage of rats acting strangely, or working in concert for a common goal that wouldn't make sense for rats to want or need.

Our best guess was that Rat King was the unknown-not-shipment that had come in on the ship Susan had informed us of. Of course, the next question was how no one managed to notice an insanely giant rat on board. Or his zombie rats either. I mean, I know ships are warrens of corridors, but where would those fit, let alone hide?

Virgil had sent Greg back to the city to fly around again, keeping an ear out for him. As no further reports other than the jewelry thefts had come in about the Rat King, Virgil was guessing he was currently hiding out in the sewers or abandoned warehouses. He was too big not to be spotted if he was wandering the streets themselves. Even at night someone should've noticed something. Although maybe I was wrong. Greg keeps telling me people aren't that observant.

Then a call came in from one of Virgil's "clients" so to speak. Someone had jumped their fence and was prowling around their property, and they didn't want to call the police because they had some "sensitive" types in the house.

"Code for their dealers," Virgil told us.

"Drugs?" Ranger asked, amused.

"Art," Virgil said. He turned to me. "Will you be okay? I've got to go deal with this."

"Yup. Make sure to use the no-kill trap."

Virgil chuckled before heading to his garage. I could hear the rumble of the Cobra below us from where we were sitting in the living room.

Ranger looked at me. "No-kill trap?"

"Half the time when they call Virgil about this stuff, it's a raccoon," I said without looking up from the book of MC Escher art I was flipping through. I didn't want something I needed to pay attention to, and this was the closest to coffee table books for display Virgil had.

"What is it the other half?"

"A squirrel."

Ranger chuckled. "Seriously?"

"I think he got a call for a crow once," I said. Ranger's shoulders were shaking. I eyed him. "Are you alright?"

"Virgil doesn't seem like the type to put up with being a glorified exterminator. All types of crime stopping aside."

I shrugged. "It pays the bills. And it lets him snoop around their houses with impunity."

Ranger was grinning at me. "I think I like Virgil."

"He grows on you," I said, going back to the book.

"What about you?"

I sighed and closed the book over my fingers so I could save my place since he seemed determined to continue the discussion. I had been trying to avoid conversation with him since he had pointed out he thought I was flirting. "What about me?"

"You seem like this would be - I don't want to say below you per se, but yeah. Below you."

I snorted. "And what would you know about me that would give you that impression?"

"Oh, I don't know, the constant assertion that you don't

have time for this shit—"

"That is not constant—"

"The comments about dumbass decisions—"

"Yeah, well people make a lot of them—"

"The headstrong refusal to play politics—"

"Because they're a waste of time—"

"And you don't have time for that shit. I know," he was still grinning at me, leaning forward, arms resting on his knees. It was a real grin, the kind that reaches the eyes, not the sideways smirks he was always giving.

I felt my lips twitch, and I had to fight not to smile back at him.

But the smile had fallen off his face, his eyes had gone distant, head tilted to one side. "That's—" he said.

"What?" I uncurled from the couch, placing my feet on the floor. He didn't answer, just held up a hand, listening to whatever it was he could hear. "What?" I repeated impatiently.

He finally snapped back to himself. "Downtown, Rat King." He was getting up, looking at me. "Are you coming with me?"

I scrambled the rest of the way off the couch. "I'm not staying here by myself if that thing is rampaging around. Where? When? I'll text Greg."

He was silent, the distant look back. "Huge park, somewhere with," he paused, "Slides, swings, somewhere with kids. Within the next, maybe the next hour? That part isn't clear." He closed his eyes, head cocked back to the side. "There's a zoo?"

"Ford Harris Park," I said, typing out a quick text to Greg and almost dropping my phone when Ranger grabbed my arm to pull me toward the garage. I wasn't even sure if I had gotten the text sent.

"We have to go now; we're going to be cutting the timing close," Ranger hadn't let go of my arm, my phone still dangling in my fingers. I snatched at it with my free hand to tuck it into my pocket, giving my arm a yank so that he released me.

We raced down the stairs, and Ranger went ahead of me to grab his bike. I paused by the stairs to pick up one of the extra garage and gate remotes Virgil was now stashing by the entry. Ranger had started the bike, the engine already growling.

"Get on," he said. I hesitated. "You'll be fine. If we wreck, I'll just reverse us. Easy peasy." I hesitated again. "Meg, you either get on the bike, or I leave you here."

I clambered over the back of it, my hands on his shoulders. He grabbed them, wrapping them around his waist. "You try to hold on like that you'll fall off. Tight grip, I'd rather have a bruise than lose a passenger."

"You just said—"

"I know what I said. You want to fall off anyway? Because you'd still feel it, and it hurts."

I grit my teeth. "No."

"Then hold on." He revved the engine, released the brake, and the bike shot forward. I was clinging to him, my chest pressed to his back, legs squeezed up against his.

The sound of the engine was echoing off the tunnel walls, and I could feel one of Ranger's hands on mine, hitting the remote for the garage ramp. The bike came up, and was airborne for a moment as we exited the garage, then the tires came down. I buried my face against his back, the scent of leather in my nose. I was sure I was about to be grateful for Virgil's driving.

Ranger's hand was back on mine, and I could hear the metallic clanking of the gate as it rolled out of the way. It wasn't going to be fully open before we reached it.

I felt the bike tilt to the side as he turned it to steer through the gap.

I might have squeaked.

Ranger chuckled. Then we were through, flying up the road, headed for the city.

We reached downtown without incident, but now we

were stuck in traffic. When we had to stop at yet another red light, Ranger planted his feet, stood up, looked around, then sat back on the bike, bringing one leg up, the other keeping us balanced.

"Hold on," he said.

"I am holding—" I started to snap, but he revved the engine, the tires squealing against the pavement. Then the bike was speeding up the space between cars, whipping by side mirrors. I ducked my head back down against Ranger, my arms squeezed around him.

A gust of air, and the cars barreling towards us in the intersection slowed, Ranger steering us between the bumpers, so close they were almost brushing against my legs.

I'm definitely never complaining about Virgil's driving again.

He took a corner, the bike tipping so low I could've reached out and slapped the pavement, but I was more worried about not dying. Also, would that result in road rash or would I lose a hand trying a stunt like that?

He jumped over a curb and was speeding down the paved trails of the park, dodging pedestrians, gusts of air flowing as they reversed people out of our path.

The bike skidded to a stop. We were outside the zoo entrance, a lion, tiger and peacock on the welcome sign. All three glared down baleful and menacing. The peacock had too many eyes.

I could feel my arms trembling from a mix of adrenaline and exhaustion from gripping so tightly. "Why are we stopping?" I asked him, pulling out my phone. Damn it, the text to Greg was still waiting as a draft. I hit send and put my phone away.

He held up a hand. "Near," he cocked his head, "I'm trying to get a sense of the exhibit, but it's – God damn it."

There was screaming. I clambered off the bike and ran. Ranger made a grab for me and missed.

"Meg! God damn it, Meg, wait up!"

I could hear Ranger racing after me, but it was the screams that mattered. I called the whispers, and they came, figures flowing along the path, rustling the rose bushes that lined it, shadows rippling along the pavement. I followed the curve of the path, and almost ran straight into the Rat King. I stumbled to a stop; with a shriek, it turned to face me, its tail whipping through the air.

And I was in the way.

I ducked, one hand raised uselessly for defense as the figures slashed at it, but they're no good for blocking something with that kind of momentum. I registered a gust of air before the thing slammed into my raised arm and shoulder, the impact knocking me into the air. Someone yelled "Shit!" And then I crashed into the rose bushes.

The whispers brushed against me, the figures swirling, shadows billowing as they circled me. It's weird the things you register when your brain hasn't quite caught up to what just happened. My hand and arm felt like they were on fire, the searing racing up the limb to throb with my heart, and I could feel the pricking of the thorns, a branch digging into my back. The sweet smell of the roses. The sun above me. But what wasn't there was sound. There should have been the rustling of the branches and leaves as the figures eddied among them, the yelling and shouting of the other people in the park. Even the shrieking of the whispers was absent, the silence making my heart pound in panic.

And then it came rushing back; the whispers screaming, the roaring of the Rat King. He was out of my range, and the whispers had chosen to stay by me. I could hear Ranger swearing. I needed to figure out how to get out of the bushes, but I was afraid to shift my arm. For a brief moment when I had been airborne and my body had registered the pain, I had flashed back to a derelict hospital, the squeaking of a cart being wheeled inexorably closer to me. I couldn't afford to be there now, not when I needed my mind here, where the danger was.

The ground shook.

There was a different kind of roar, mingling with the shrieking of the Rat King. Thuds and more ground shaking, the sounds of bodies rolling and scuffling. And then, finally, the Rat King's strangled screaming before there was a wet tearing noise.

Silence.

Greg's voice. "Meg! Meg!" The figures and the whispers withdrew, shaking the branches and leaves, shedding rose petals that brushed against my face as they spun down. Greg's face was over mine, his arms reaching in to pull me out. His face and arms were speckled with blood, and it was soaked into the shoulder of his shirt.

My hand and arm were throbbing too much for me to protest that I was fine. I could feel it in my collarbone too, the ache deep in the line where the bone had knit back together. I could feel each scratch the thorns had caused burning along my skin, which seemed particularly unfair when I was pretty sure I had another broken bone. Or, you know, five.

I was trying to move my arm against my chest, and I mewled when I started to lift it. Then Greg's hand was on it, his grip gentle but firm, shifting my arm, cradling it so he didn't scrape the fracture against itself.

He swung me away from the bushes toward Ranger's voice. "Hold on, I can help—"

"I think you've done enough of that," Greg snarled.

"If you would wait, I can fix—"

"I don't want you fixing anything. This wouldn't have happened if you hadn't dragged her along with you. Stay away from her." Then the rushing of air as Greg took flight.

∞

We arrived at the compound at the same time as Virgil. Greg landed in front of the Cobra as it came up the drive before it could reach the ramp down. Virgil came out of the car, leaving the door open. "What happened?" he demanded.

"Rat King," Greg told him. "Ranger took her with him."

Virgil's hands were on my face. "Meg. Meg, look here. Focus on my fingers. How many am I holding up?"

"Three," I said, my voice a whisper, my arm and hand still throbbing. Virgil's hands had moved and were hovering over me, his brow furrowed.

"The only bad injuries are the arm and the hand. The rest are just abrasions. Get her inside. I'll get the car moved and then get them set."

Greg took off down the tunnel and up the stairs. Ranger and I had left the bookcase open, so he landed us inside Virgil's room. He marched me down to the lab, set me down on the hospital bed, and pulled up a stool next to me. He was holding my good hand in both of his. One of his thumbs rubbed back and forth across my palm. I turned my head to face him.

"Hi," I said weakly.

"Hi," he said, giving me a smile. I could see the shadow of anger in his eyes.

I might not be a fan of Ranger, but no one made me get on that bike. And Greg should know I don't let anyone push me into anything.

"He didn't drag me."

"Meg," Greg sighed. "I don't think—" but he looked away from me toward the door.

Virgil's boots, the footsteps stopping by the bed. "Meg, this is going to hurt. I can give you—"

"No!" I said, a spike of panic. Greg squeezed my hand. "No drugs, please," I managed more calmly.

"Local anesthetic only, no drugs that affect cognitive function," Virgil said reassuringly.

"Oh," I said. My heartbeat slowed.

"Ready?" Virgil asked.

∞

Greg had planted me in our bed as soon as Virgil was done getting my arm and hand set and into a neon pink cast. Which he did on purpose because I hate neon and the eye-searing effect it has.

Plus side to having a telekinetic as your doctor: manipulating bones back into place happens right the first time, and you don't need to bother with x-rays either.

As soon as Greg had me settled, he left the room, closing the door behind him, and it wasn't long after that the shouting started.

Being me, I got my ass out of that bed and headed for where the shouting was originating from. I crept slowly down the hall because I didn't want Greg to hear my footsteps.

"What were you thinking leaving her here with him?!" he was yelling.

Virgil was shouting back, which surprised me. I had never heard Virgil yell before. "I was thinking she can handle herself! He's not a danger to her!"

"Well obviously he is! Dragging her off to get—"

"I highly doubt he dragged her anywhere! Meg got on that bike of her own free will, or we would be cleaning what's left of Ranger up off the living room floor!"

And the walls, and the ceiling, and the – you know what? You get the point.

"You—"

But Virgil had gotten steam, and if there's one thing you don't want to let happen with Virgil in an argument, it's let him get ahead. "I what?! I understand that she's capable! I watched her for *years* while you all completely underestimated her!"

I was at the door of the lab, and I could see just past the doorway to where Greg was bristling because the argument had turned. "I didn't underestimate—" It was a good thing his back was to me and he was concentrating on Virgil, who was out of my line of sight.

"No, you didn't. Shockingly, you didn't do what the rest of them did, and ignore just exactly what she could do to get a signing bonus," Virgil snapped. "But what was the first thing you *did* do when they asked you to go talk to her? You asked her out! How is that any better?"

"That is not the point!" Greg roared. "She shouldn't be—"

"Yes, she should be!" Virgil was shouting back again. "Meg did exactly what she should've done when she was the only one on this team left here and got information about a villain! She alerted you! And then she took what resources were available to her and went to deal with it!"

"She wasn't outfitted for—"

"She rushed off without thinking. She does that," Virgil's tone had steadied. "Talk to her about that. But stop trying to stuff her in a cabinet to keep her safe. Since when has she responded well to anyone trying to control her actions? And if you keep trying to constantly shield her, you will lose her. She can handle herself out in the field, and she can handle herself against Ranger being a prick."

I could hear Greg grinding his teeth. "Ranger—"

"Ranger is not the problem," Virgil said firmly before Greg could start shouting again. "I know what the problem is, and I think Meg has made it clear to him she's not interested in whatever he has to offer. If it gets to the point where Meg wants help getting him to back down, she'll just murder him anyway."

That surprised a chuckle out of Greg. "That's not—" he paused, rather than finish that thought. He sighed. "I don't want her to feel pushed to that point."

"Stop rising to his jockeying to get close to her attempts and she won't be. If she thinks you're willing to let her handle her own shit, she'll be more likely to come to you for actual help. And then you can pound him into the ground."

Greg had a hand in his hair, and there was a long silence. "I haven't told her," he finally said.

"What? That you love her? I think she knows." Nice, Virgil, nice way to skate past the part where you told me.

"That's—" Greg made a frustrated noise. "Every time I go to tell her, we get interrupted. I want to make it clear to her how I feel, but Ranger's constantly there, popping around corners."

"Well, don't do it here. That's hardly romantic."

Greg laughed. "I'm not sure she's a fan of the romantic. I tried that. We ended up eating takeout on a rooftop."

"So do that. Go get tacos from a food truck. Take a walk in the park. Should be safe enough now that you won't have a giant rat showing up. But if you have to keep pulling that thing out of your sock drawer, she's going to spot it before you're ready."

My heart dropped. It hammered in my chest and stomach simultaneously because I most definitely wasn't ready for whatever Greg was hiding in his sock drawer, and now that my heart was pounding like it was, I needed to retreat before Greg noticed it. Except I turned to go, tripped and hit my newly broken arm on the wall. I bit back a yelp and jerked away from the wall, my good arm trying to cradle the other side.

"Meg?" Greg's footsteps. "Meg, are you alright?"

"Fine," I snapped, tears in my eyes. Stupid broken arm.

"What are you doing out of bed?"

"I wanted a soda," I said, because it was the first thing I could think of, "so I was going to the kitchen."

"Hmm," Greg was watching me like he didn't believe me. Which since I was facing entirely the wrong way wasn't surprising.

The callbox buzzed from the security room before he could argue with me. Virgil came out of the lab, steering around both of us. We followed him, and I was grateful for the interruption. A sigh from Virgil. "It's Ranger." He hit the intercom. "What?"

Ranger was sitting on his bike at the callbox. He held up the remote so we could clearly see it on camera. "I'm only hitting the box to be polite. Let me in, or I'm coming in anyway."

Virgil hit the button for the gate.

"You're letting him in?" Greg was growling again.

"Yes, I'm letting him in," Virgil said. "He has my remote." We watched Ranger come through the gate and open the garage. Virgil turned on his heel and went into the hall. "If you're done overreacting, I'll be in the living room."

Greg was tense next to me, his coiled energy tight enough that he was almost vibrating, and I couldn't figure out what I wanted to do. Act normal? I was worried he would sense something was wrong, and the timing to distract him was way off. Plus, broken arm. He would know something was up. I hesitated, and then started when he wrapped an arm around my waist. He paused, his arm slipping back.

"Are you alright?" he asked quietly.

Heavy footsteps were coming down the hallway, and now I didn't want the interruption.

I grabbed Greg's hand with my good one, interlacing my fingers in his. "Fine," I said. "But you need a shower."

He looked startled and then looked at his arm. It and his face were still speckled with blood. Some of it was in his hair, and he was still wearing the bloody shirt.

Ranger paused in the doorway. "Am I allowed to be near her yet?" he said, his voice acidic.

"I think that's up to her," Greg said, his tone cool, his fingers tightening briefly on mine.

"Great. Meg, let me see your arm."

"Why?" I asked, stepping and turning so that my back was pressed against Greg.

"Because if your attack dog had just listened, I could've reversed the damage. Now I don't know if I'm still in the time limit," he snapped.

Behind me, Greg was silent for a moment, then shifted his feet, and cleared his throat. I twisted my head to look up at him. He had one hand on the back of his neck, eyes downcast on the floor. "Sorry," he said, although it sounded somewhat grudging. He cleared his throat again. "I might have overreacted. Meg, can you let him look?"

I hesitated, still pressed against Greg.

"Clock's ticking," Ranger said.

Greg settled his free hand on my hip and gave me a gentle nudge forward. "Let him look, please."

I grumbled, holding my broken arm out as much as I could. Ranger grabbed it with one of his hands, and I hissed. Greg's fingers flexed in mine. "Sorry," Ranger muttered, the other hand hovering over the cast. His eyes had taken on that blank look. "Yeah, it's going to be close." He shot a look to Greg. "You uh, might want to hold onto her. This is going to hurt."

I started to protest, but Greg had let go of my hand and wrapped his arms around me, pinning me to his chest. "Hey!" I yelled.

Ranger hadn't let go of my arm, I could feel the twist in the air and felt when my bones unset themselves. I screamed, trying to yank my arm back and kick free of Greg at the same time. Then with a scraping noise I could feel the bones rejoin. If anything, that hurt more. I howled. Then Ranger had let go of my arm and I snatched it back against me.

It had stopped hurting, but now I was pissed. I shoved away from Greg, who let me go, and then both of them tried to catch me when I staggered. I slapped their hands away, my hand stinging from where I had smacked Greg with it.

"Don't touch me, either of you!" I spat. "That fucking hurt!" I stomped out of the security room toward the living room. "Virgil, get this cast off me!"

CHAPTER NINE

I had ended up retreating to our room, and then I sat there staring at the dresser, trying to decide if I wanted to toss it for whatever was hidden in there. I had time to go looking for it because Greg had come in to retrieve clean clothes before he went to shower, but I didn't know if I wanted to confirm what I had overheard.

But my arm and hand weren't broken anymore, so I had that going for me.

The door opened, and Greg came in. He looked at me, still sitting on the bed glaring at the dresser, and sighed. "You're still mad?"

"No," I said, because otherwise he would hear the lie. Saying yes might have been easier, but I wasn't sure if it would be one of the times where he would let it slide.

He sat down on the bed next to me. "What did the dresser do to deserve your death glare?"

"Nothing." Because the dresser hadn't done it.

He wrapped an arm around me, and I tensed. He pulled his arm back. "Are you alright?" he asked me quietly.

No was the answer, but I couldn't tell him that, and I couldn't hurt him by telling him I wasn't ready for the same step he was. Instead, I switched topics. "Why were you and Virgil arguing?"

Greg cleared his throat. "No reason."

I narrowed my eyes and transferred my glare to his face. "It didn't sound like the 'no reason' kind of shouting."

He hesitated.

I hopped off the bed. "When you decide you want to tell me I'll be in the kitchen."

He grabbed my hand. "Meg—" he paused. Sighed. "We were arguing about you."

"About me what?" I snapped.

He looked at the floor and muttered something.

"You're going to have to speak up because I don't have super hearing."

He brushed his hair back with his free hand. "About me being overprotective of you."

"Hmm," I said, since technically I knew what the argument was about. "Virgil took my side didn't he?"

"Yes." Greg sounded irritated.

I smirked at him. "He tell you I can rescue myself?"

"He called you capable."

"That's almost like a compliment coming from him."

"Yeah, well, he also said you rush off without thinking, so don't let it go to your head."

"I do not—" I started to argue, then paused because I did tend to do exactly that. "Damn it."

"Yeah," he pulled me to him, and I went, settling back down on the bed next to him. "Promise me next time you'll at least stop long enough to get some sort of protective gear on."

"Okay," I said. Although there was a very good chance I would forget in the heat of the moment.

He heard it in my voice. "You're going to forget, aren't you?"

"Probably," I said.

He sighed, wrapping his arms around me. "Meg—" he started, and I kissed him. He responded, one hand in my hair, and then he pulled back, his hand sliding to my face. "I love you," he said softly. My heart sped up and skipped a beat at the same time. I was frozen in place, staring into his eyes as they lit up, and for a moment I was terrified of what he would say next. But then his lips were back on mine, and for a while, I didn't have to think about how to say the words out loud.

∞

It was always the sand and the sea, the olive grove above us. For a while we, the whispers, figures, shadows and I, walked down the beach. The sand soft beneath my feet, heavy skirt dragging it along behind us.

We climbed the hill the grove sat on, trading sand for the pricking of grass and sun-warmed dirt. The bark of the trees was rough under our hands. We plucked ripe fruit from their branches, eating the flesh and leaving the pits dropped on the ground behind us as we wove our way on a path only we knew.

"*Megaera.*" A messenger on the wind. This time we would have to answer lest we offend him.

He had always been quick to anger. We had that in common. We all did. Petty were we.

I kept trying to remember. They should be coming, the memories. But try as I might, they kept slipping away.

Had we made a mistake?

∞

I was awake, in the dark. Greg was still asleep beside me, his breathing deep and steady. I rolled to look at the clock. It was three in the morning, but now I was wide awake. I sat up, sliding off the bed and padding quietly out of the room. I didn't want to wake Greg.

I headed for the kitchen. I would get a glass of water and then head back to bed. The light in the kitchen was already on, and I assumed it was Virgil. He kept odd hours sometimes. Often, I wasn't sure when or if he slept.

But when I stepped into the kitchen it wasn't Virgil in

there, it was Ranger. He was straightening up from the fridge, a soda in his hand. He was shirtless, and I felt my face redden, like I had walked in on something indecent. I started to back out of the kitchen, determined to go down to the bathroom to get water from the sink there.

But he had already spotted me. "Yo," he said. "Can't sleep either?"

I paused, hesitating, caught between continuing my retreat and acting normal, which would involve making a smart-ass comment and then retreating anyway.

He popped the top on the soda and set it on the island at the edge closest to me, and then he got a second one out of the fridge. He opened that one and had sat down at the island before he said anything else.

"You going to sit?"

I stepped forward, and when he didn't move, I crossed to the soda he had left me and sat down, slowly turning the can in circles.

Sometimes, when it's quiet like this, I can hear the ocean waves in my ears. But they keep getting fainter when it feels like they should be getting louder.

At first, we sat there not speaking. Normally I would be the one to break the silence, but Ranger did it first.

"Do they do that often?" he asked, and it sounded like a question he had been chewing on for a while.

"Does who do what?" Question for a question, because if he wasn't going to be clear from the start, I wasn't going to help him.

"The things, with the fingers," he said. "Any time I see them around you, they're touching you. But when Susan was here-" he went silent for a moment. "How often do they put those around your throat?"

I shrugged. "Often enough." Greg had noticed too, but he could hear what the whispers were saying when they wanted him to, and whatever they had said he had found reassuring. The figures couldn't help it anyway, their fingers were just too long.

"Are you at risk from your own power?" Ranger demanded.

I snorted. "No."

He must have found something blasé or dismissive about my attitude. Which, yeah, honestly, I was being dismissive. "This is serious," he said. "People who can't control their power have died. One of them took out an entire town when they did." His voice had risen, and I could hear anger and frustration in his words.

I turned my head to look at him. "I'm not in danger from them."

"From your power," he corrected,

"No, from them. They're my power."

"That's – you talk about them like they have a mind of their own."

"Because they do."

"That's not possible," he insisted. "Powers don't work that way."

I shrugged. "Mine does."

He was silent again for a long moment. "Is that why you were all so difficult about letting me in?"

I smirked. "No." Took a sip of soda.

It was literally just because we're difficult. Okay, fine, I'm difficult. We had managed to settle into our own little team groove, and Ranger's appearance was a disruption to the routine we had established. Greg's very core might be based in protecting people, but Virgil was our glue, the leader, our director.

I'm the snarky comic relief, and there's only room for one of us in this town. Ranger was friction we didn't want.

Or maybe he was friction I didn't want, and Greg and Virgil were reacting to my emotions, my level of stress, and without me in the picture, things would be going smoothly among the three men.

Relax, I'm not going to bounce. Just musing.

Ranger had finished his soda, so he got to his feet and headed for the other side of the island where the recycling bin was. With the way he was moving, I could see his side where long, thin raised scars ran along his ribs, curving around toward his chest.

He saw where I was looking and pointed at me with the can. I saw the flash of a matching scar down his arm. "You did that."

"Not sorry," I said, taking a sip of my soda. Normally I would be curious about how he had managed to heal so quickly from it, but now I knew. What I was curious about was why it had scarred. "Is it normal for that to happen?" I asked.

"Is what normal?"

"The scars. I thought you could reverse the damage."

"I can, and no, it's not normal."

"So, you didn't just come here because your power can't affect them."

Another long silence from him. He was watching me, his dark eyes unreadable. "No," he said finally. "And not just because of the scars either."

"Why then?" I asked.

"I was curious about you."

"Hmph," I snorted. Because I doubted I could be that fascinating to someone who had just met me. I tend to rub people the wrong way on first impressions. Weird, right?

"You weren't the least bit curious about me?" he asked.

"Nope," I said. "I don't do mystery."

"So, you think I'm mysterious?" he grinned at me.

"Not really," I said, but his grin just widened, and from the knowing look he was giving me, he didn't believe me.

"How'd the attack dog manage to catch you?"

"Excuse me?" The sudden subject change to Greg left me wary.

"How long did you play hard to get with him before he finally caught you? What did he do?"

When had Greg caught me?

He had already had my attention at the point it happened, luring me in with a steadfast, patient refusal to let me get myself killed. He had kept insisting on protecting me even when I continued putting myself in danger out of a blend of pettiness, overconfidence, and a stubborn streak a mile long.

But he caught me when he gave me his shirt.

Ranger was still waiting, leaning forward with both hands set on the countertop.

"He gave me the shirt off his back," I said.

"I don't have a shirt," he said, smirking.

"Wouldn't help you anyway," I said.

"How sure are you about that?"

"Absolutely positive," I said. "You don't stand a chance." I hopped off the stool leaving my half-finished soda there, and I left him in the kitchen, those dark eyes on my back as I went out the door.

∞

When I wandered back into the kitchen later that morning, Virgil and Greg immediately stopped talking. My 3:00 am wandering meant I had slept late. The soda was gone from the counter, and I didn't know if it was Virgil, Greg or Ranger who had cleared it. At my entrance, Virgil suddenly became very interested in his coffee mug, and Greg was studying his feet. And that put me on alert.

"What?" I asked suspiciously.

Greg busied himself pouring me a cup of coffee and sliding it over to my usual spot on the island instead of answering.

I didn't move from the doorway. "What?" I repeated.

"You're blocking the door," came Ranger's voice from behind me.

I shot him a glare over my shoulder before heading to the island and sitting down. Greg and Virgil cleared away from the coffee pot, but they both left the island between us. Ranger had poured himself a cup of coffee before anyone spoke up.

"I think," Virgil said, "that Ranger and I could handle anything that comes up, if you needed to take a trip home Greg."

I narrowed my eyes at him. "You and Ranger?"

Virgil didn't answer me, just watched me over the rim of his mug as he took a sip.

Ranger seemed to realize he was currently caught in the middle of planning he hadn't been a part of, and he wasn't going to cooperate. "If Greg's going home, wouldn't it be you, Meg and me?" he asked.

Greg set his mug down in the sink. "My mom invited the two of us to dinner."

"What, us two?" Ranger asked. "Because I've got plans already."

Greg shot him a look, but apparently he wasn't going to rise to the bait. "Meg and me."

"When did she do that?" I asked, wary of people making plans without me. I didn't know what the two of them were discussing right before I came in, and I had my suspicions that it had something to do with whatever was in Greg's sock drawer.

"This morning," Greg said. "So, I hadn't had a chance to talk to you yet. I wanted to make sure Virgil would be okay with us taking the time off."

"If it's just dinner, why would we need time off?"

"Because my brothers are invited too, which technically means the invitation is to stay for the weekend," he said.

"You can fly. Why would you need to stay the whole time?" Ranger sounded irritated. "You and Meg could just come and go."

Greg chuckled. "Yeah, I'll explain to them why I'm bailing on the family events. That'll go over really well."

Rangers scowled but didn't answer.

Greg leaned back against the counter. "Meg?" There was a hopeful note in his voice, and I could see that Ranger caught it too because his eyes narrowed. It looked like he was measuring his chance. He would let go of it eventually, right? How many times and ways did I need to tell him I'm not interested before he gets the point? Flirting misreads or not?

I grabbed my coffee and hopped off my stool. "I better not have to pack anything fancy," I said and headed back to our room, ignoring the grin on Greg's face and Virgil's crinkled eyes, who I knew was hiding his smile behind his mug.

∞

I'm not sure what I was expecting, but Greg's mom definitely surprised me. She was tall, like her sons, whose resemblance to each other was unmistakable. Her coloring dark where theirs was light, and she had Greg's dark brown eyes. She was warm, friendly and inviting. Until you tried to help yourself to the dinner rolls, apparently.

She had set them, fresh from the oven, on the table, and Peter, the middle child, had immediately reached across the table for one. She had smacked his hand away. When Tony, the oldest, also tried to reach for one, she smacked him upside the back of his head. "Guests first!" she chided.

"Ma, aren't we technically all guests at this point?" Tony protested.

"Family doesn't count as guests. Meg counts as guests," she said, moving to sit down at the head of the table.

For a moment, everyone at the table stopped talking to stare at me. Which included Tony and Peter's wives and Greg's six nieces and nephews of varying ages. I could feel my face redden. You already know I'm not a center of attention kind of person, and this was too much attention.

Greg chuckled and grabbed a roll.

Tony protested again. "Ma!"

Greg dropped the roll on my plate.

"How come he doesn't get smacked?" Tony demanded.

"He was serving Meg," their mom said calmly.

Peter rolled his eyes. "Come on, Ma, we all know it's because you'd break your hand."

"Pierre, no hero talk at the dinner table," she said.

I stared down at my plate to keep from breaking into giggles. I don't know what Greg's parents were thinking when they named their kids. Look, I know mine isn't much better, but at least my parents had, like, reasoning, or a theme or something.

"That's not hero talk," he grumbled. "Asking about the bridge, that's hero talk. And what was with the monster in the park? News said you ripped its head apart at the jaw?" He was dishing out potatoes. Apparently, the roll on my plate was the signal everyone was waiting for, and now food was being passed around.

"Pierre," snapped their mom.

"Peter," he corrected her.

"I gave birth to you; I'll call you whatever name I want. Thirty-eight hours of labor—"

"And I got stuck. I know, Ma."

Tony interrupted the brewing argument. "What do you do, Meg? Greg's been tight-lipped about you."

"Hero work," I said, half-apologetically.

Their mother sighed. "I'm never going to get grandbabies."

"Ma!" Tony and Peter were motioning at the kids at the table.

"You know what I meant," she said.

Their wives, Brit and Sandra, were steadfastly ignoring the conversation going on between their husbands and mother-in-law. Maybe it was a common theme, the arguing and the ignoring. Until one of them smacked the table and pointed at me.

"I knew I recognized you! You're the one from the bank!" Brit said.

The table was suddenly silent again. Greg slipped a hand onto my leg, warm and reassuring.

Tony cleared his throat. "Brit, no hero talk at the table."

Their mother floundered for a moment, then latched onto a different topic, but it wasn't any better than the bank. "What about your family, Meg? You have any siblings?"

"No," I said.

"You see your parents often?"

I raised my chin. "No, we don't have a relationship." I sure as shit wasn't going to explain any further.

That stymied her for a moment. "Oh, well. The boys don't have a relationship with their father, God rest his soul."

"Dad's not dead, Ma," Peter said.

"He is to me," she said. "Who wants ham?"

∞

After dinner, his mother and sisters-in-law disappeared to the kitchen with the leftovers and dishes. The kids went racing off somewhere outside, at least I thought. It had sounded like a door off the kitchen had slammed shut, but no one had given me a tour, so other than the entry and the dining room, I had no idea what the layout of the house was. I stayed trapped at the table because Greg's arm was resting across my shoulders, and I couldn't have gotten up even if I wanted to. Peter was waxing eloquent on something about interest rates and historical lows and that it would be a great time for Greg to buy a house.

Greg was leaning back in his chair, and he might have looked relaxed to his brothers, but I could feel how tense his muscles were. "I'm not in a position to buy a house," he told Peter.

"You can't tell me that financially—"

"I'm done discussing it."

"I tried to tell you going freelance was a bad idea," Tony told him.

"That's not the problem."

"Meg, are you the problem? Greg not buying a house

because you're too picky?" Peter asked.

I opened my mouth to retort, but Greg sailed right in. "Also, not the issue."

Tony snorted. "Then what? You've got to grow up sometime. If it's not money, not your girlfriend, what's your excuse?"

"I don't want a house," Greg snapped. "I can't just go settle in a neighborhood. It'll endanger everyone around me."

Greg's mother sighed from the dining room doorway.

"Told you, Ma," Tony said. "You can take the man out of the hero, but you can't take the hero out of the man." His voice held a trace of a sneer and something else that I couldn't place. He pointed a finger at Greg. "You're breaking Ma's heart because you're the baby, and you're still not settled. You should find yourself a nice, normal girl, retire and settle down. No offense, Meg."

"Because that worked out so well for Mom and Dad," Greg said.

There was a heavy silence.

Greg's phone rang. He muttered and pulled it out. "Timing," he grumbled when he answered it. The scowl on his face cleared, changing to bewilderment, "What? It was, yes, I'm sure it was dead! I know how to tell when something is dead!" He had straightened up in the chair, "Where now? The big one in Flex Square? No, you and Ranger go ahead, we'll meet you there." He hung up and was already standing up, pulling me to my feet. "We have to go."

"What happened?"

"Apparently the Rat King isn't dead."

We seemed to be having an issue with things or people that should be dead not staying dead. Speaking of, I wonder how Mirage got home. I hope he had a really, really long walk and that he didn't get his nose set straight.

Tony, Peter, and their mother were staring at us stone-faced. Greg sighed. "I'm sorry, we have to go."

"It's fine," his mother said, "Your father was always

racing off to save the world too."

Greg led me out the front door, and shut it gently behind us. He pulled me to him, his nose in my hair. "Hold on," he said. I wrapped my arms around his neck and buried my face in his chest, my feet standing on his. And then we were in the air.

CHAPTER TEN

He landed us at the edge of the square, set back from the fountain in the center. In the lights surrounding it, I could see the Rat King in the fountain itself. It was, as far as I could tell, empty of people, although I thought I had caught a flicker of movement in the shadows all the way across the courtyard from us. Greg set me down but blocked my path with an arm, pulling me back from the streetlamps.

"What?" I hissed.

"Where are Ranger and Virgil? They should've beaten us here."

I looked around. We were crouched just within sight of the fountain, the shadows before the streetlamps cloaking us. Greg's arm tensed against me. "I hear squeaking," he said.

"Zombie rats," I said. "I'll get them, you get the big one."

He turned his head to look at me. For a moment he was silent, worry in his eyes. "Watch yourself," he said, before kissing me and launching himself at the Rat King.

I stood, pulling the whispers to me, and began stalking through the shadows. The figures swirling around me, I pushed them outward, and they eddied, flowing through the air, the shadows spilling over the ground in their wake. I could hear the figures' fingers scratching at the bricks beneath my feet. I circled with them, searching around the perimeter of the square for the rats Greg had heard.

To my right I could hear roaring, splashing, and the clatter of flying masonry as pieces of the fountain got knocked away.

Squeaking and scurrying to my left, and I turned to face a wave of zombie rats ten times larger than the horde I had taken down in the Sung building. The figures billowed, diving into the rats who screamed as they burst, entrails and blood tangling up the ones coming from behind them. But they kept coming. I was backing up; the blood seeping toward my feet was a viscous, rusty red, and I didn't want to be stepping in it.

Except now the shadows and I were in the light, and the Rat King saw us.

The figures were churning the air around me, rising and crashing like waves as they circled, and the Rat King left off his battle with Greg to charge me.

Caught between him and the horde, the whispers screamed, and I darted to the left, as the Rat King hit the edge of the shadows. He reared back shrieking.

And then he was yanked away from me. He slammed down into the bricks, and I could see Virgil across the square. Greg dove at the Rat King, and I could see him pounding into the thing's chest, hear the snapping of bone. It was screaming but couldn't fight back because Virgil had it pinned to the ground.

The shadows rose around me, swaying like snakes in the grass. The zombie rats were still coming, and there were a lot of them. Then the figures were flowing forward to meet them; there were more screams and the wet popping of their bodies. But there were so many of them, and I couldn't move forward to meet them if I didn't want to be stepping in the blood. I had to wait for them to come to me.

They had realized I had a range, and they circled me, settling just outside the shadows standing guard around me. The light was reflecting off their eyes as they sat there, watching me. I took an experimental step forward, and they scurried back, staying just out of reach of the whispers. There was intelligence driving their actions. The zombie rats weren't just the mindless henchmen of the Rat King I thought they were.

This was going to be a problem.

There was a movement to my left, and I turned to look.

Ranger, and he was - when did he get a baseball bat? He had clocked the rats in his way across the head, and they were just as vulnerable to that as they were to the figures. Their heads shattered, spraying bone and brain matter.

The shadows withdrew just enough that Ranger could step into the circle they had formed, and then they converged on the rats that had tried to surge forward. Ranger staggered toward me, away from the free-for-all going on there, shadows flowing back outward, figures seething in the air.

The whispers giggled in my ears. The figures seemed uninterested in him now that he was in the circle itself. Or was it because I had told them they could trust him not to hurt me?

"Yo," he said. "Need a hand?"

"When did you get a baseball bat?"

"It was in the Hummer."

"Okay, why do you have a baseball bat?"

"For the zombie rats."

"Obviously," I said, lips twitching.

"You got a plan, Stan?"

I pulled the figures to me, and the rats charged. "Let's play ball?"

Ranger chuckled and started swinging. The figures boiled forward to take out the rats trying to leap at him, swirling and curling as they would brush by me before flowing back out into the rats. The whispers were laughing and howling with glee.

The rat horde scrambled back out of reach, the figures eddying in a slow circle around us. There was a surprised squeal, and then a rat smacked into Ranger's back. He staggered forward, twisting, but the shadows had already billowed around it, smearing it across the pavement as the figures came rushing back only to surge back outward when the rats tried to press forward. Both of us stepped away from the spreading pool of blood.

"Oops," Virgil called.

The whispers giggled. Until the rats turned as one quivering mass to look at Virgil and Greg, a sea of glinting eyes. "Throw another one!"

Virgil did, a flick of his hand and rats went airborne, popping like balloons, their remnants raining down on the others when they hit the edge of my range and the wall the shadows had created.

At that point the rats tried to swarm us, and my focus changed, narrowing to the ones the figures could spill over onto, reaching with their long fingers to drag the ones that got too close into our space so the shadows could crash down onto them. I could see Virgil making rats burst with a wave of his hand. Greg, unfortunately for him, was having to get physical, and by the time we were done he was covered in the gore.

Ranger and I stood in the only clear spot, a circle of clean brick. I let the whispers go.

Greg came striding through the blood and bodies, stepping up to me. "You okay?"

"Not even a scratch," I said.

"I'm good, too, thanks for asking," Ranger said.

I saw Greg's eyes flick toward him, and then they were back on mine. "I'd offer to take you back to the compound, but I don't think you want this stuff on you."

"Nope. I get covered in that shit too often as it is."

Virgil was clearing a path to us with a sweep of his hand. "As adorable as the two of you are being right now, I want to know why it wasn't dead."

"Maybe there was more than one?" I suggested. "Or it had babies?"

"Perish the thought that that thing was breeding in our city."

Ranger was studying the rats, quiet for a change. "What if it's not the rats?"

When he didn't elaborate Virgil sighed. "Meaning?"

"When I was in Havana, I spent a couple nights with a woman who could talk to animals." The look Virgil shot him I would classify as skeptical. Greg, on the other hand, snorted. "What? I get around a lot," Ranger said.

"Like Dr. Doolittle?" I asked, smirking.

"You're hilarious. Yes, like Dr. Doolittle. You'd like that power, Virgil, they're great for gathering information. The birds love to talk."

"Your point being?"

"Maybe we're dealing with someone like that. I mean, she couldn't get the animals to follow commands, or you know, mutate. But…"

"A shockingly observant thought and not outside the realm of possibilities," Virgil mused. He was giving Ranger one of his long, considering looks. "And if he hasn't been mutating the rats until after he came over, there wouldn't have been any reports of this to compare the events to." He was silent for a moment. "Okay, Ranger, Meg, in the Hummer. Greg, we'll meet you at the compound. I have to put out some more feelers on this."

"Shotgun," I said.

Virgil eyed me. "Excuse me?"

"You heard me; I'm taking shotgun."

"I thought you didn't like my driving."

We were headed toward the car, Greg trailing with us. "It's growing on me," I said.

Beside us, Ranger snorted. "You mean you found someone's driving you like less."

"That was not driving," I said. I was pulling open the passenger side door, Greg standing as close to me as he could without brushing gore off on me. I looked up at him.

"Don't get that shit on my car," Virgil snapped from the driver's seat. Ranger was climbing in behind him.

"I'll see you at home," Greg said, eyes serious.

"Yup," I said.

"I love you," he said, and my heart sped up. He smiled, stepped back and took off.

"Meg," Virgil was saying, "get in the car."

I climbed into the seat and shut the door, my heart pounding.

"Seatbelt," Virgil ordered, the Hummer rumbling to life. Automatically, I reached back and got buckled in.

Eventually I was going to have to say the words out loud. Greg would want to hear more than just the beat of my heart.

I could feel Ranger's eyes watching me on the ride back.

∞

Greg was already inside and in the shower when we got back. Virgil snapped his room door shut behind Ranger and me as soon as we had headed into the hallway.

Which left me with the choice of hiding in my and Greg's room, or socializing with someone who had followed me too closely up the stairs.

What? I need, like, five feet between me and everyone else at all times. It's my bubble; I get to decide where it ends.

If Ranger asked me what his chances were right now, I would literally throw something at his face. I could feel his eyes on me while we stood awkwardly in the hall for a moment, and then I headed to the kitchen. I didn't want to make Greg feel like I was hiding from him by retreating to our room. If Ranger wasn't here, the kitchen or living room would be where Greg would usually find me. I mean, unless I was in a snit. Which was why if I was in our room, he would think I was hiding from him. The thought gave me pause. When had I started caring about upsetting anyone about where I choose to sit and how they interpret that?

I grabbed a soda but didn't open it. Instead, I sat at the

island, occasionally turning the can in circles, listening to the aluminum rub against the stone. Ranger leaned back against the countertop by the sink, arms crossed, watching me.

"Rat got your tongue?" he asked eventually.

"No," I said. I popped the can open and glared at it, thinking. Greg hadn't mentioned his dad had been a hero before he left. It had been bugging me since dinner, and it felt like a safer subject to concentrate on.

Also, no wonder he doesn't talk to his brothers much. Tony's kind of a bossy, nosy asshole. Peter wasn't too bad, just incredibly boring.

"You're not usually this quiet," Ranger tried to get my attention again.

"Maybe I just don't have anything to say," I snapped. I was trying to think over the events during dinner. Damn it, we had left our stuff there, and I got the feeling Greg didn't want to go back to spend the rest of the night with them. Not that I minded not going back.

If anyone was even awake. What time was it anyway?

Ranger's voice in my ear: "Things getting too serious with the attack dog?"

I jerked, knocking the soda over. "Jesus, bubble! Out!" I slid off the stool to go get towels, putting space between us. His voice had held a note of either curiosity or concern, but because I had been lost in thought, I hadn't noticed his approach. Now I was as angry at myself as I was at him.

"You okay, Meg?" Greg was in the doorway, leaning on the frame. The look on his face was dark. If he had been looking at me like that, I would've been scared. It made me think of the time he flipped the table.

Speaking of – who got stuck cleaning all that up?

I tossed the towels onto the counter and pointed at Ranger. "That was your fault." I stalked to the door, Greg twisting to let me pass through. I headed for our room, and after a moment, I could hear him follow me.

Virgil would be glad nothing in his kitchen was about to

get broken.

Greg closed the door behind us, surprisingly soft, the click of the lock.

I stood in silence, glaring at the floor.

"Do you need me to handle him?" Greg asked.

"No," I said, swiping at my face. Do you have any idea how annoying it is to be a crier when you're angry? Everyone thinks you're sad about something when really you just want to murder them.

"You sure?"

"Yes," I snapped, finally turning to look at him. He was leaning back against the door, watching me. "What?"

He stepped up to me, hands hovering. I could feel the heat from his body. "Meg," he said, and my heart sped up. I could read the words in his eyes.

"I know," I said, locking eyes with him. But I could see doubt lurking in them, and that hurt, and I was already pissed off. "Don't you dare!" I shouted, startling him into stepping back. "Don't you dare doubt my heartbeat! You're not misreading me!" I could hear the whispers sighing before they faded.

He hadn't moved, but his lips twitched. The doubt had left his eyes. "You don't need to yell it at me," he said.

"Apparently I do," I said, because yelling it at him was the best he was going to get from me right now.

I don't have commitment issues; I have expressing that level of commitment issues. Don't act like you always tell people how you feel.

He chuckled and stepped back up to me, putting one hand on my face. "You can yell that at me, in any form you need to, at any time you want to. And I won't doubt you."

"Good," I said. And then his lips were on mine.

∞

We, the whispers, figures, shadows and I, were in the

olive grove, the sea below us, and we prowled along the path only we knew, down the slope through the trees.

He was waiting for us on the beach, the scent of brine so strong in the air you couldn't tell where the sea ended and he began. His hair was still wet, straggling, stuck to his face and neck. There was a storm on the horizon, crawling lightning and circling clouds. A prison? Our prison? But the thought was gone, receding with the waves.

"My brother is looking for you," he said.

"You aren't usually his messenger," I replied. I didn't know why he had come, if it was a warning or a threat. I had gone at the last call, hadn't I? But the memory of why he had wanted me was forgotten.

He was saying something else, but the wind whipped the words away. I couldn't ask him what he had said, because he was bleeding away, his form foaming back into the sea.

There was only the sand, the sea, the olive grove and me. Our memories had faded again.

Would we ever remember, or would we only forget?

∞

Greg's phone was ringing. I covered my head with a pillow and heard the rustle of the sheets as he rolled over. "Hello?" he said. His voice was still thick with sleep. I felt him sit up. "Where? What time? How many?" He sounded much more alert now, and I pulled my head out from under the pillow.

"What?" I asked.

But he was still listening. "Yeah, no, we're on our way. Give us an hour? Absolutely, whole team." He hung up.

"What?" I was getting tired of repeating myself.

He was scrubbing at his face. "That was Detective White. They're on their third jewelry store theft of the night, and each time, it's been rats."

I sat up. "Like, the zombie rats or the rat rats?"

"Just the rat rats apparently. They aren't tripping the alarms until right before they leave." He got up. "I've got to wake up Virgil. Get dressed. She wants all of us down at the precinct." He shut the door behind him.

I slid off the bed, grabbing clean clothes out of the dresser and hesitated, hand hovering at one of the top drawers. I turned away, pulling on a shirt, skinny jeans, socks, and knock-off chucks.

What? Why should I pay name brand prices?

I headed out the door and almost stepped directly into Ranger, who dodged around me. "What's going on?" he grunted.

"More rats."

"It just had to be rats."

"Better than snakes," I said, but Virgil and Greg were coming past us to head into the security room, Virgil tapping something out on his phone.

"Meg, can you go make the coffee? I've got to finish this message, and then we all need to figure out how we're getting to the precinct to see what our Rat King did this time."

"We're still going with that name, huh?" Ranger asked.

"Yes," Greg said stiffly.

Virgil headed into the room, Greg leaning against the wall of the hallway, glowering at Ranger. Ranger glowered back.

Greg's phone rang again. He pulled it out, looked at the screen and sighed but answered it anyway. "Hey, Mom. No, the problem is ongoing. I'll be by later to pick up our luggage. No, we can't come back to stay right now."

I slipped into the kitchen to do as Virgil requested. 4:00 AM wake ups for everyone was going to require so much coffee.

Ranger followed me in and leaned against the countertop next to me. I was busy pulling out coffee beans and getting the grinder going, so I ignored him. The whispers were at my back, figures and shadows sliding on my skin. Ranger took a step back.

"You can just tell me I'm in your space," he said.

I shot him a glare and turned back to the coffee pot. "You're in my space," I said.

He backed up farther. I let the whispers go and hit the "brew now" button. I stepped around the island so I didn't have to pass right by him.

"Did I do something to piss you off?" he asked.

"Don't know why you would get that impression."

He had moved, so he was blocking my path out. "You don't need to be sarcastic."

I flared up. "Obviously, I do. Because you're not getting the hint."

He was watching me, dark eyes shadowed and unreadable. The tension was stretching, rising, on the cusp of breaking, and a beat before he moved toward me, I could sense it. I dodged backwards. The moment broke, and he backed up. I was left wondering if I had misread the situation. Still, I darted out of the kitchen for the security room and the safety of Virgil's company. I could hear Greg in the living room, still on the phone, but if I went in there with my heart hammering the way it was, he would go murder Ranger, justified or not.

I was going to have to go nuclear if I wanted Ranger's interest in me to stop. I'm not into loud, public declarations of "I'm unavailable and in love," so I had no other ideas on how to tell him he had no chance. Since I had straight up already told him he had no chance. Multiple times.

What? Vaguely yelling at him is the same as if I told Greg I love him. It counts. Shut up.

Virgil looked up from his phone when I came in. He took in my flushed face and waved a hand. The door to the room slammed shut. "What do you need me to do?" His tone was sharp.

"Are you done with your testing?" I asked, skipping around the subject.

"For now," he said, his brow furrowed. "Let me think about this. He's useful and I don't want to alienate him completely. But if he keeps trying to step in between the two of you, Greg's going to lose his temper. Or you will."

"Why do you think he'd lose his temper before I would?"

"Meg," Virgil half-sighed, and he sounded scolding, the volume of his voice louder than usual, "you let Mirage stalk you for two years. The only time I've seen you take anyone down was when they were an immediate threat." I started to protest, and he continued, his voice softened. "I'm sorry, that's not how I should have phrased that. I'm not saying you're wrong, and I'm not blaming you. Your restraint is a valuable part of you. Especially with your power. And while I would prefer to keep him as an asset, if Ranger isn't listening when you tell him you're not interested, I will tear him limb from limb if you don't do it first." He went back to his phone, finished typing out his message. "If you would go get Greg for me, we need to get going as soon as possible."

I opened the door to the hallway; Ranger was hovering outside. "Move," I told him. He backed up.

I slipped past him and headed toward the living room. Greg was coming into the hallway. "Virgil wants you," I said.

"Hmm," he said, slipping an arm around my waist, and I fell into step with him, headed back to the security room. "I could hear him all the way down the hall."

We went in, Ranger behind us, and he hung back at the wall by the door.

Virgil looked up at us. "What are you doing in here? Go, Ranger and I will meet you there. I'll bring the coffee pot. You don't want to drink what's available at the station."

Greg narrowed his eyes. "I thought you wanted to see me."

"Did I?" Virgil said. "I don't recall saying anything like that."

Greg sighed, his arm still on my waist as he steered us out the door past Ranger. We walked down the hall, through Virgil's room and into the garage where Greg snagged a remote for the ramp.

He pulled me up against him, and paused, looking down into my face. "Where's the Kevlar?"

"The Hummer," I said. "Do I really need it? It's just the precinct." I could see him weighing it, the hesitation in his eyes. I reached a hand up to his face. "I'll be with you."

"In my sight the whole time?" he asked.

"The whole time. Won't move from whatever spot you stick me in."

He chuckled, and then took off up the tunnel, while I hid my face against his chest.

CHAPTER ELEVEN

He landed us on top of the precinct roof itself, setting down back from the edge. He set me down, but didn't let go of me, keeping me pressed to his chest.

"What are we doing?" I asked.

"Waiting," he said.

"For what?"

"For Virgil and Ranger to get here."

"We should've brought the coffee pot."

He chuckled, his nose buried in my hair. "We could go pick up breakfast after. By the time we get done, the coffee shops should be open."

"Hmm. For just us, or are we including Virgil?"

"We don't *have* to include Virgil," he said. He was silent again for a moment. "If Ranger doesn't give you space, I don't care what Virgil thinks, I'm going to break his jaw."

I pulled my head up, leaning back to look at him.

"Meg," he sighed. "This isn't about you being able to rescue yourself. I know you can. And—" he scrubbed at his face. "His, his intentions aren't—" he made a frustrated noise, like he couldn't figure out how to explain what he was trying to say to me. "I don't think he realizes that he's making you feel hunted."

I stayed silent, waiting, trying to think back over our conversations, because I had been stressed and irritated by his interest. But hunted?

Greg was continuing. "Which doesn't excuse his

behavior. And I'm trying to let you handle it, I am, but I really am going to break his jaw if he keeps it up." I opened my mouth but he kept going over the top of whatever protest I had. "No, Meg. Today was the last straw. I heard the way your heart spiked, and if you hadn't already gone running to Virgil for help," he paused, took a breath, "The last time I heard your heart do that you had a panic attack."

But I had gotten distracted from the conversation. I was in the kitchen, and he had been on the phone. How did he even know?

I think he saw the question on my face. "Meg, I could pick your heartbeat out in a crowd of thousands. It might take me a minute, but I would find you."

It was oddly comforting to know that. I would never be lost in the woods as long as we had each other. Not that I go out to the woods.

Greg tilted his head to the side. "I can hear the Cobra. They're almost here." He scooped me back up and took us over the edge in one bounding leap, landing in front of the precinct doors. Virgil pulled up to the curb almost sedately.

Ranger was climbing out of the passenger side, and when he saw us, he dropped his eyes. Virgil gave him a hard pat on the shoulder as he strode by him.

"Good talk," Virgil said. Ranger shot him a look but didn't say anything.

We went inside, and Iver, the desk sergeant, looked up. Did this guy ever go home? He had already picked up the phone and was calling White to tell her we were here. Guess we were on the highly anticipated list at this point.

White came striding down the hallway, her cheeks flushed and shiny, like she had run most of the way here. She paused when she spotted us, her eyes on Ranger. Then they flicked over to Greg. "Fortress. Didn't realize he was one of yours."

"He's not," Greg said.

"He's one of mine," Virgil said. Ranger looked just as

surprised as White, but he covered it more quickly than she did.

"White, this is Vigilante," Greg said. "I take it you've met Ranger," he added glossing over the fact that we knew she had met him before. Now that I think about it, as far as I know, Virgil never removed that tracker from Ranger's bike.

"Ah, Vigilante. Well, that explains it then," White said, reaching a hand out to shake Virgil's. "I heard you had started your own team."

"Did your resource happen to be an intrepid reporter?"

"Maybe," she flashed him a grin. "She got very irritated when I didn't have any information to trade her for that tidbit she let drop."

"I didn't realize my team status was so interesting to people," Virgil said.

"I think heroes who choose the private sector are always interesting," White said. "I like to know where their funds are coming from."

I saw Virgil's lips twitch. "You aiming to go further than robbery, White?"

She leaned onto the counter of Iver's desk. "I've always found forensic accounting fascinating."

"Hmm," Virgil said, the corners of his eyes were crinkled. "A path for an analytical mind certainly."

Was – was Virgil flirting with her?

Well, he did say he doesn't date heroes, but he never said cops were off the table. Although Virgil tended to skirt the line of what is and isn't legal. Or, you know, jump right over it. So maybe dating a cop wouldn't be on his radar.

White turned to look at Iver. "You call Mason? He wanted to be in on this."

"I thought Mason transferred to Homicide?" Virgil said.

Greg looked startled. Virgil must not have shared that information with him.

"He did," White said. "This time, your Rat King killed someone."

"He's not *our* Rat King," I said.

148

"Whomever the Rat King belongs to," White said. "Now we've got a dead jewelry store owner."

"When?" Virgil asked.

"I'd like to wait for Mason," White paused. "Here he comes."

Mason was coming up to us at a jog. "Jesus, Iver, a little warning would've been nice," he snapped. "Now we've got heroes *and* monsters to deal with?" He was looking our group over. "How many heroes does it take to take care of a God damn rat?"

"You didn't see the size of this thing," White said.

Mason grunted. "So fucking show me."

White motioned for Mason to precede her, and he grunted again. "Conference Room A-One," she told him. He started off, and we fell into line behind them. We walked down the hallway, past interrogation rooms, past what looked like where they were booking people, and up a set of stairs. Mason shoved the door to the conference room open, and we all filed in. White headed for the AV equipment that had been set up. Instead of sitting, we all stood gathered a few steps back from the TV and cart. Mason grunted and stepped over to one of the tables, leaning back on it.

"Do you mind?" Virgil asked, the offer in his voice.

White turned her head to look back at him. A flick of his hand and the TV was on, and a startled White had stepped away. Whichever video she had gotten in was up on the screen playing already. Virgil's arms were crossed with one hand up as we all watched. Virgil was fast forwarding through the video up on the TV; a flick of his hand, and it went back to playing at regular speed. The footage was grainy and dark, but you could see dozens of rats climbing the cases, working at the locks, and then carrying pieces of jewelry off. Some of them were dragging necklaces along the floor, the chains trailing behind them.

"Is this one just a robbery?" Virgil asked.

White joined Mason at the table. "Yes. This was the first tonight."

Mason was jiggling his foot. "Show them the one that has me *concerned*."

White moved back to the stand, switched out the DVDs, backed up, and Virgil flicked his hand again. When the security tape slowed, it showed a man, standing behind one of the counters, working on paperwork.

"What time was this one?" Greg asked.

"Midnight," White said.

"When did the call for it come in?"

"At—" White started, but Mason made a shushing noise, as he pointed at the screen.

Rats were streaming into the store, and they attacked the owner, scurrying up the legs of his pants, swarming over him as he screamed and tried to shake them off. They were biting and scratching at him, and I took a step back from the screen, my heart speeding up, as I watched the owner fall and disappear beneath the teeming pile of packed bodies. You couldn't hear the sound, thankfully, but you could tell he was still screaming, as his body struggled and eventually slowed to twitching before the only movement left was that of the rats.

I don't watch horror movies for a reason. What I can do myself is bad enough to see. I've still got some human empathy in there, somewhere, and no matter who you are, watching someone get eaten alive by rats is disturbing.

Greg had slipped an arm around my waist, pulling me against him, his voice warm in my ear. "Vengeance," he said.

Yes, the whispers said. Greg straightened up the slightest bit, but the whispers had faded, so his arm tightened back against me.

White and Mason had both focused on the location of Greg's arm. Or maybe they were focusing on the fact that I had leaned into him, taking the comfort he offered in that moment.

"Huh," Mason said. "Don't do that shit around Dulle and Howell."

White snorted. "Yeah, like they would notice."

"It's off the record," Virgil said.

"There's more than one intrepid reporter out there," White said.

"You said there's at least one more robbery?" Virgil asked, as the video continued to play. The rats had moved off the body of the store owner and were back to their regular operations of opening the cases.

"Yes—" White said.

But Ranger, who was being uncharacteristically quiet beside us, stepped forward interrupting her. "Pause it! Pause—" But Virgil had already paused it and was looking questioningly at him.

"What?" he asked. "What do you see?"

Ranger pointed. "The mirror, what's in the reflection?" When we all stared at him, he smirked at us. "That's your Doctor Doolittle."

We all crowded forward to take a closer look. Virgil sighed and turned his head. Greg and I backed up. "Thank you," Virgil turned back to the TV. "Is that – it looks like a person? Vengeance first, look at this."

I stepped up to the TV, concentrating on the mirror at the back of the store that was just within sight of the camera. With the way it was angled, it was reflecting whatever was outside the front window on the sidewalk: the vague smudge of a figure standing there, watching the rats work. I stepped back. Greg moved in.

"It definitely looks like a person," he said.

"So, when the rats are there, he has to be nearby," Ranger said.

"It would appear so," Virgil mused.

"So next time they show up, we need to search the surrounding area for him," Greg said. "And take him out."

"Piece of cake," Ranger said.

Mason and White were studying the screen now.

"So, our Rat King is a human?" White asked. "Not the giant rat?"

"That would be the current working theory, yes," Virgil

151

said.

"*Giant* rat?" Mason asked. "The swarm of rats isn't enough here?"

"And zombie rats," I said.

"Zombie rats," Mason said slowly.

"Yeah, they're like ROUSs but, grosser," I said helpfully.

"What the fuck is an ROUS?" Mason said.

"*Princess Bride*," Virgil said. "Vengeance watches a lot of movies. Just ignore the references."

"Excuse me," I said, "but pop culture is my bread and butter."

White snorted.

"If we could stay on point. That thing," and Mason jabbed a finger at the screen. "Just murdered someone, using a swarm of rats. And you're planning on waiting for him to just show up?"

"We've been trying to locate him, but we were operating under the assumption that the giant rat was the Rat King."

"What would a giant rat need with jewelry to start with?" Mason demanded. "Why wouldn't you look for a person from the beginning? How is the rat going to get rid of the jewelry? How's he going to sell it?"

"You're assuming the end game was to generate funds," Virgil said.

"That's why people steal shit to start with!"

"Regular people," Virgil said. "Not villains. Sometimes they do it just to have the collection."

"No," Mason said. "That's where people who operate like you do come in. They buy the stolen shit so they can collect it without getting their hands dirty and then claim they didn't know when we come calling to get the shit back."

"Black market," Virgil said.

"Yes—" Mason started to snap at him, but Virgil had pulled out his phone and was texting a message, his fingers flying over the screen. Mason looked at us, then back at Virgil. "What is he doing?"

"We've been assuming that the Rat King was just collecting and holding the jewelry, like a hoard," Virgil said. "I need the manifest of all the stolen items, please."

"One minute," White said, and she headed out the door. She was back moments later, files in hand, and she set them down on one of the tables. Virgil stepped up, flipping open the files, and reading through the items. He turned his head to look at White and Mason.

"Do you mind?" he asked. "I'll need to send these lists to a contact of mine so she can tell me if any of those items have come under her purview."

"Is your contact a fence?" Mason asked nastily. "Because I want a name."

"No," Virgil said. It was unclear whether he was answering the question or refusing the demand.

White waved a hand at the files. "Go ahead."

"Thank you," Virgil said, and held out his phone taking scans of the lists.

"You're—" Mason started, but White interrupted him.

"Yes, I'm going to let him send that to his contact. He just said she's not a fence. Needs must," she said. So now we know which way White chose to interpret that.

"Done," Virgil said, closing the folders. "Is there anything else? Anything to do with the third robbery tonight that's unusual or different from the others?"

"The murder to start with isn't bad enough?" Mason sneered.

"No," White said, skipping by Mason's opinion. Cold pragmatism maybe, but who I am to tell someone else how to express their feelings. "Same as all the others: no murders, no giant rat. Or ROUSs."

Virgil held out a card to White. "In case anything unusual or different does happen." She took it, slipped it into her pocket. "Team," Virgil said. He headed for the door, and we followed.

∞

Once we were outside and standing by Virgil's car, Greg spoke up. "I was going to take Meg to get breakfast."

"I know a great little diner off of fifth if you're interested," Virgil said. "I'll drive."

Like he would let anyone else drive that car anywhere. Greg and I climbed into the back, me behind Virgil and him behind Ranger. Unlike when Mirage was stuck with Greg behind him, Ranger did not hunch himself up, but he definitely looked like he was brooding.

Traffic was still relatively light for a city the size that it is, so Virgil made the trip to the diner a quick one. Yeah, he hit the gas pretty hard in front of the station, hard enough that the tires took a minute to get traction before the Cobra shot forward.

The cops probably didn't chase him because they had tried that before and it didn't work out so well for them. I'm not sure who Virgil paid off or threatened after the fact with blackmail, but that chase made national news, and people were laughing at the cops for weeks after. I do know that no one got hurt and that there was shockingly no property damage either. This was years ago, because Vigilante's been a Malus City fixture since I was a kid, so you would think Virgil might be more circumspect now.

You know, I should ask Virgil about it.

We had been silent on the way there, Greg's hand resting on top of mine the only reason I kept from making any comments. Once Virgil had pulled up at the curb, Greg climbed out before me, and offered his hand back to me. Because my knee had chosen to pop at that moment and I saw the way his lips thinned, I took the help.

And I saw the way Ranger's eyes had flicked to our hands and away.

Down the sidewalk from us it looked like they had blocked off the street. There were vans and cameras, boom mikes, and people milling around with walkie talkies. All four of us paused to watch for a moment, my hand still in Greg's, and he slipped his free arm around my waist again.

"Another movie?" Greg asked.

"Yeah," Ranger said. "There, they're setting up for a dolly shot." We all looked at him. "What? I've been around Hollywood a couple times."

"Hmm," Virgil said. "Well, some day you can tell us all about your exploits. But for now, let's go eat and discuss our Rat King now Pied Piper."

"Yeah, you think I'm planning on hanging around that long?" Ranger asked.

"Oh, I know you are," Virgil said, as he sailed past the rest of us into the diner.

Ranger looked bemused, like he knew Virgil was right but had no idea how Virgil had managed to come to the conclusion he had. The rest of us followed Virgil into the booth he had selected. Greg and I slid in across from him, Ranger next to him. Ranger seemed to be trying to avoid meeting my eyes, choosing instead to either look at the table or stare down Greg.

A waitress came around and handed us menus. Her name tag read Barbara. "Hey, hun, haven't seen you in a spell. Coffee?"

"Yes. Might as well bring a couple pots," Virgil said.

Greg was looking at the menu, flipping it over. "What do you cook the eggs in?"

"Lard," she said. "But if you have dietary restrictions, the cook will fry them up in something else. Let me get that coffee for you, and you can let me know what you can't have." She walked away.

"Thought we were sticking with Rat King," Ranger said.

"Hmm, Rat King, Pied Piper, same difference," Virgil said, who was also perusing the menu.

"I think, according to history, they're two very different tales," Ranger said.

"Both villains either way," Greg said. "At least he's only stealing jewelry and not kids."

"Yeah?" Ranger said. "I thought the Pied Piper did that because he didn't get paid."

"Who do you think sent the rats into that town in the first place?" Greg asked.

Greg's mention of kids made me think of a question I didn't want to ask, but now I needed to. The last time he had appeared, the Rat King had been in the park. "Should we be asking White and Mason to pull any recent missing children reports?"

All three of them focused on me.

"Fuck," Virgil said. He pulled out his phone. "Greg, what's her number?"

"On it," Greg said, already texting.

Virgil made an irritated noise. Greg looked up at him, then back down at his phone. He sighed. "I'll have her send them directly to you."

"Thank you," Virgil said.

We were silent now, staring down at our menus. I don't know that any of us had an appetite anymore. They never found the kids in the original tale. No one knew precisely what happened to them, but based on what happened to the store owner, I think we all suspected if we had a new Pied Piper out there, it was nothing good.

Barbara came back with two carafes of coffee, four mugs, a container of cream and a bowl of sugar packets. "Y'all know what you're getting?" she asked as she set the items on the table.

"I think just the coffee for now please, Barb," Virgil said.

"Bad night, hun?"

"In a manner of speaking," Virgil said. She nodded, and walked away again, headed behind the counter of the bar.

Ranger ended up pouring coffee for all of us because the three of us hadn't moved. Then he leaned back against the cushions of the booth, one arm resting along the top of it, hand on the mug still sitting on the table. Virgil, Greg and I were all hunched forward for another moment, before Greg leaned back, leaving both his hands on the table. Virgil had his elbows up on the table, mug between both hands, his brow furrowed.

My own eyes were on my cup, glaring at it.

Ranger, despite having been so quiet, was the first one to break the silence. "Is that your signature look?"

I flicked my eyes up to his face. "Is what my signature look?"

"You spend a lot of time glaring at inanimate objects. Your face is going to freeze like that one day."

"I already have RBF, so not much will change," I said.

He smirked at me, but from the way Greg and Virgil were shifting, he had changed the mood, and maybe that had been his intention. Now he changed who he was addressing. "So, what's the plan once we hear back?"

Greg scrubbed at his face. "We need to find him and take him down, quickly."

Ranger snorted. "Yeah? How, genius? How many jewelry stores can we stake out at once?"

Virgil interrupted before it could turn into an argument. "We look for a pattern." He had pulled his phone back out and set it in the middle of the table so we could all see. He was flipping through the scans of the missing property lists. "Where are these stores located in relation to each other? What are they near? What did they have in common, other than being jewelry stores—" his voice had risen because Ranger had opened his mouth, probably to make a smart ass comment. "Did they all sell a specific designer? Stones from a specific region? Were they all individual stores, or part of a chain?"

"How does that help us?" Ranger asked.

"If he's operating from a central location in relation to these stores - and taking children from that same area - we should be able to triangulate about where he is."

"Huh," Ranger said.

"Not used to having to operate on only bits and pieces

of where you need to be, are you?" Virgil asked.

"No," Ranger said. "Not used to monsters and demons either."

"Not a demon," I said. "And they're not demons either."

"I feel like someone who steals people's kids for any purpose might qualify as a demon," Ranger said.

Well, I couldn't argue that. And it was nice that he hadn't intentionally poked at me because I thought he had meant the whispers.

Virgil's phone pinged and vibrated in the middle of the table, and he snatched it up. With exaggerated care, he set the phone back down in the middle of the table. I could feel Greg tense next to me.

"It's not good, is it?" he asked Virgil.

"She said two a night, since the store thefts started. Mysterious ones, where the kid has just left the apartment. For the ones that have security cameras, the kid just goes out the apartment door, down the elevator or stairs, and then disappears right after they get out the front door. Can't track them up or down the street."

The table groaned, from where Greg's hands were resting on it. He pulled them back and cleared his throat.

"Shit," Ranger said softly.

The whispers were in my ears, hissing, and now Virgil and Greg had tensed for a different reason. I shook the whispers off, and they faded. "Sorry," I muttered.

"Hmm," Greg said. "I think I'd be more worried if they hadn't shown up at that moment."

I gave him a weak smile, but to do that, I had to turn my head, and now I was looking out the window. The parking meters at the street had all bent in half. I shot a look at Virgil, who looked back at me, the picture of innocence.

"What?" he asked.

I'm pretty sure Virgil regularly downplays how powerful he really is. I don't think he needed that paintball gun for tag at all.

And I think he knew I suspected something because he cleared his throat. "White is supposed to be getting me the names and addresses, or at least getting Ross to send them over to me, since they're his cases."

"Why wouldn't they say something to start with?" Ranger demanded. "That seems pretty important."

"Different department," Virgil said. "And they don't always communicate well."

"Rat King is gonna cause a turf war over there," Ranger muttered.

"So definitely Rat King?" I asked.

"It's just easier to stick with what we're already calling him," Ranger pointed out. "Less confusion."

"I agree," Virgil said. "And we should eat. Rather than take up one of Barb's tables."

I looked around; we were currently the only customers. Virgil leaned forward, his voice low and quiet. "She's keeping the place clear so we can speak freely without a bunch of civilians asking nosy questions."

Oh. Barb had a modest power. Another type of compulsion, a small command essentially: not here, try somewhere else.

Virgil waved her over, and she came out from behind the bar. "What'll y'all have?" she asked, all smiles.

Our meal was a mostly silent affair, for our table at least. After Barb had taken our orders, people started to drift in, and the place had filled up pretty quickly.

Based on the food, it was no wonder it was so popular. That or Barb could also invite people with her power. But I didn't ask; she wasn't harming anyone, and Virgil was already aware of her.

When we stepped outside of the diner, they were still working on whatever movie they were filming. Virgil and Ranger had already stepped up to the car.

"Are you coming?" Virgil asked.

"I'll take Meg back the other way," Greg said. Virgil nodded, and he and Ranger climbed into the Cobra and took off, Virgil pulling an illegal U-turn in the middle of the street. Greg snorted. "He could've just used the intersection before the barriers."

"I don't think that would be on brand for Virgil," I said. I was watching the commotion; there were so many cameras and people. I hadn't realized how much went into just the physical action of putting a movie together. Greg had an arm around my waist again, his nose in my hair as he kissed my head.

"Did you want to watch them film for a bit?" he asked.

"Do we have time to waste watching them?" I tilted my head back to look up at him.

"And you say you aren't the heroing type," he chuckled, sad and tired as it was. But he had put a hand in my hair, bending his face to mine, and kissed me, soft and sweet. Then he pulled back, straightening up, looking around.

"What?" I asked.

"I thought I heard..." his brow furrowed, but whatever it was he thought, he didn't see. "Come on, we should go. Once Virgil has the addresses of everything, he's going to be pulling out maps and making us all stare at them until we go cross eyed." And he scooped me up and took off.

CHAPTER TWELVE

We beat Virgil and Ranger back to the compound, going in through the garage since Greg had one of the remotes. Once we were in the living quarters, Greg started prowling around from the kitchen back to the living room.

"What are you doing?" I asked. His pacing was making me nervous.

"Virgil's going to need space to spread the maps out. I'm trying to figure out if he's going to just use the island or if I should move the furniture out of the way."

"Well, pick a project because you're making me anxious."

For all the tech Virgil has around, you would think he wouldn't do some things in such an old-fashioned way, but he says sometimes you need the hands-on method. I don't see how using the internet is less hands-on but whatever.

Greg stepped up to me. "I'm making you anxious?"

"Yes," I said. He wrapped his arms around me, pulling me into him, his nose in my hair as he took a long, slow breath. "Do you just like the way my shampoo smells?"

He chuckled, but he didn't answer the question. He straightened up. "They're back."

I had heard the rumble under our feet of the Cobra as it came into the garage, so I would've known even without Greg's hearing.

Virgil came striding into the living room, steering around us to get over to the bookcases, where he went straight for the section farthest to the left, pulling books off and piling them onto the coffee table. Except once he had them out and on the table, I realized they weren't books at all. They were accordion folders, disguised with leather binding.

Should've known Virgil would be concerned about the aesthetics.

He opened one, unlocking the latch on it, and pulled out maps, checking something on them before setting some of them on the table and stowing others away.

Ranger had paused at the entry into the living room itself and was watching us watching Virgil. "Does he do this often?"

Ranger hadn't seen Virgil in research and destroy mode before.

Greg was the one who answered him. "Often enough."

Virgil's phone pinged, and he pulled it out, pointing at the drawers set into the bottom of the bookcases. One of them opened, and a pad and pencil floated over to him. He was looking at his phone, left floating in the air while he wrote down whatever it was he was looking at. He tore the slip of paper off, grabbed one of the maps off the table, and held them out.

"Meg," he said, "take these, I need you to highlight the addresses on this list. Greg, Ranger, don't move, I'll have some for you in a minute."

Greg let go of me, and I crossed over and snagged the papers from Virgil's hand, went to the drawer of the bookcase, grabbed a yellow highlighter and spread the map out on the floor. I heard Greg sigh, because my knee had chosen to pop while I got settled.

"If she's comfortable..." Virgil said absently, the majority of his attention still on what he was writing down.

I was busy running my finger down the streets, crouched over the map, nose practically to the paper. I ticked off an address and went back to running my fingers along the paper. I heard Virgil rip another piece of paper free.

"Greg," he said. I heard movement as Greg grabbed what Virgil offered him, and then he came over, spreading his map by mine, so that he was crouching on the floor by me.

"Ranger," Virgil said. More movement and rustling of paper, and then Ranger was on the floor, having spread his map out across from Greg and me. I heard Virgil unfold another map and set to work on his own, and then we were silent except for the rustle of paper, the sound of highlighters sliding across the maps.

I was done first, sitting back from my map, stretching my arms and neck to get the crick out. Virgil snatched my map up from the floor, went over to one of the blank walls, and stuck it up there, no tape. Then he was back at his map, searching. When Greg sat back from his, he repeated the procedure, and then again for Ranger's. He marked one last address on his, and that map joined the others.

He stepped back from the wall. We were looking at a completed map of Malus City instead of the sections we had each been working on. Based on how spread out our highlighted sections were, I didn't think we were going to find a pattern.

Virgil swore, but he had his hand up at his chin - classic Virgil thinking pose. He stepped back up to the maps, muttering as he looked them over.

"There are clusters," Greg said.

"I see them," Virgil said, "but they don't seem to have any relation to each other. If I consider the clusters as the locations, we still end up with the entire center of the city."

"Why not the center of the center?" Ranger asked.

Virgil tapped the map. An intersection of streets was at the center of the city, clear of buildings. The only other thing there was a subway entrance. "He's in the subway!" Virgil paused. "He's in the subway and using the tunnels."

"That's not good," Greg said.

"No, it's not," Virgil said.

"There's only so many places he could be that way," Ranger said.

"No, there's a thousand places he could actually be

nesting," Virgil said. "The subway system is old; there're warrens of out-of-use tunnels down there." He was looking at the maps again. "I don't have a map of the subway systems. And we need one of all the old tunnels too."

"How is this city not a fucking sinkhole?" Ranger asked. "How does it stay up if there are as many tunnels as you say?"

"Good infrastructure," Greg said.

I snorted.

Virgil was still staring at the maps. "The main city library would have copies of the old tunnels, but they're not going to let me mark them. Same with city records. Those are originals."

"You wouldn't mark them anyway," I said. "Your heart couldn't handle it."

Virgil wagged a finger in my direction. "I need to be able to overlay the two maps anyway. See if the..." He was tracing along the maps with that finger. "Where are the subway entrances in relation to the locations he's hitting?"

"Virgil," I said, because what if these missing kids weren't the first?

"What?" he asked, turning away from the maps to focus on me.

"You said you didn't get any reports of missing jewelry or giant rats overseas. What about missing children?" The Rat King had come in through the docks, and the original Pied Piper had taken the children with him.

"You think he might be planning on leaving with them?"

"I—" and I paused because I both had and hadn't. "In the tale, he disappears into the mountains with them. We don't know if he brought any kids with him here. Where's the mountain?"

"You're assuming he's collecting them like the original Pied Piper."

"Maybe?"

"I'm not sure if that's better or worse than the alternative," Virgil said.

"Worse," Ranger said. None of us argued with him.

Virgil was pinching the bridge of his nose. "I have calls to make. Greg, please alert White that we think he's in the subway system. She needs to make sure someone over there is aware that this thing is down there and to keep an eye out for anything suspicious. And to watch the docks in case he tries to leave."

"On it," Greg said, pulling out his phone and texting.

Virgil disappeared down to his security room.

Ranger settled onto the center of the couch across from the TV, arms flung across the back of it. "So now what?" he asked. "We just sit here?"

Greg scrubbed at his face. "Well, the other option is to wander blindly through the subway and hope we find him."

"While dodging trains," I said helpfully.

"And the third rail," Greg said. "Not happening."

"They have to have ways for workers to access those places without getting hit," Ranger pointed out.

"They do. They also shut down sections that require maintenance or emergency repair, so we would still have to stick to the walls with no knowledge of where we're headed and an unknown quantity of rats."

"We could leave breadcrumbs," I said.

"You're mixing your legends," Greg said. "And what if the rats eat them?"

Ranger was leaning forward, elbows on his knees now. "If he's keeping the kids alive so he can leave with them, maybe we should go looking for them instead of him to start with. He's got to have them someplace with access to clean water or something, right? Somewhere he can reach them easily to feed them?"

"Yes, he would, well, hopefully—" Greg's eyes widened. "Gathered in a group," he said. He was scrubbing at his face again, shoving his hair back. "There's going to be whole pockets of heartbeats but—" and he darted away from us, toward the security room. "Virgil! I'm going to need a light!"

Ranger looked confused. "What did I say?"

"He can hear heartbeats," I said.

"So, he can find them?" Ranger demanded. "Why are we standing around here?" He was already off the couch following Greg.

Now I could hear arguing, so you know exactly what I'm going to do. I headed straight for the security room.

"What do you mean you're going alone?" Ranger's voice.

"I can move faster if—"

"The Hell you can! How many kids could you carry at once? We need to be able to evacuate them all in one go!"

"The weight—"

"You have two fucking hands, same as me!"

"Boys!" Virgil snapped. "We're all going. Greg, you will take point."

I popped my head around the door. "All of us?" Because I was not getting left behind to twiddle my thumbs in the compound.

I saw Greg open his mouth to protest the "all of us" plan again. Virgil saw it too. "No, Meg is coming. Her skills are too valuable to be left behind for this."

"Just your friendly neighborhood expert zombie rat killer," I said.

"I'm also worried about the regular rats," Virgil said. "You can keep us from getting swarmed."

"The fear," I said pointedly. Because Greg and Virgil wouldn't be able to be in range of the protection I could provide. Although Greg would be fine if he got swarmed anyway. And what about the kids? Being subjected to the panic I could induce seemed risky if we needed to keep them close.

"We'll just have to suck it up," Virgil said.

"I don't think that's how that works—" I started to argue, but at the look Virgil gave me, I shut my mouth.

"Are you trying to argue yourself out of going? Because we can leave you here."

"No," I said, looking at the floor.

"Good," Virgil said. "Hummer, now."

"I'll meet—" Greg started.

"No, you will not. You will ride with us," Virgil said. "I know exactly what you're thinking, and you are not going down there ahead of us. This is a team operation." He went striding past me out of the security room headed for the garage. The rest of us followed, the racket of all our footsteps echoing down the hidden staircase. Virgil had headed over to storage, while the rest of us went over to the Hummer.

Greg opened the driver side passenger door, pulled out the Kevlar outfit, and held it out to me. I sighed and took it, pulling it on over my clothes, and he helped me get it fastened and closed properly. I always have an issue getting the chest not to sit too low. Which might be on purpose because I hate things being so close and tight to my neck.

I know, you would think I would have an issue with the figures' fingers too, but they never feel fully solid.

Virgil was back, holding out those big, ridiculously bright and powerful flashlights. "Here, put these somewhere." Greg grabbed them, started to set them on the floor by the seat but paused, because Ranger had taken the rear passenger spot.

Ranger saw him looking. "What? I do not want to watch his driving any further today. This morning was bad enough. He's going to wreck us at some point."

Virgil chuckled as he climbed into the driver's seat. "I don't wreck."

"You want me in front?" I asked Greg.

"No," he growled. He kissed me, gentle despite how tense I could feel he was.

I rose up on my toes, one hand on the back of his neck so my lips could reach his ear. "You know there was no way you were ever losing this game, right? He never stood a chance," I whispered.

"Hmm," he said. "That obvious?"

"Little bit," I said, my lips still against his ear. "That couldn't all possibly be to rescue me."

"Assist," he said.

"Assist," I agreed.

Virgil hit the horn. "Get in the fucking car," he paused. "Please."

Greg helped me up and shut the door before he went around to the other seat.

"Seatbelts," Virgil said once he was in. He didn't wait for all of us to be ready before he hit the gas and the Hummer roared forward.

∞

Virgil headed for the center of the city. Greg had wanted to go straight into the first subway entrance we came to, but the rest of us agreed that if his central location was the one in the middle, that might be closest to wherever he was keeping the kids. Virgil parked illegally.

"One of these days you're going to get towed," Greg told him as we hustled out of the car.

"No, I'm not," Virgil said. Virgil had come around my open door, reaching past me to grab flashlights. He handed one to me then turned and handed two of the others to Ranger and Greg. "Do not get separated."

Ranger had his baseball bat. I looked at him. "You're not going to have any free hands."

"Did anyone tell White about this operation?" Virgil asked.

"Texted her on the way, told her to make sure Ross doesn't send anyone in," Greg said.

We were headed down the stairs, into the subway itself, commuters stopping to stare at us as we hustled down. The smart ones kept going or turned right around to get up out of the subway. See, some people are observant and realize when they see a bunch of misfits dressed like we were to run away from whatever is about to happen. Well, other than Greg, since all he wears are t-shirts and jeans. Protective gear would be pointless for him. We kept racing forward once we hit the bottom of the stairs.

When we reached the turnstiles, we all picked one, spread out in a line and jumped them at the same time. Security just watched us go by. They must not pay that guy enough because he didn't even seem to register that he should be yelling at or straight up chasing us. Look, the department of transportation is really strict about making sure people pay to use their things. So maybe they should be equally strict about making sure their employees feel well compensated. I've heard about the things people do in subways.

Oh yeah, this was literally my first time down here. I don't ride the subway trains. Just the elevated ones. Because tube, underground, people trapped in a tiny space with me if I have to use the whispers: bad idea all around.

We had reached the train platform, and we paused as a group. Greg was looking around, his feet just off the ground so he could make sure he saw over everyone's heads. He hit the floor with a small thump. "Okay, I want to go down to the left so we can see the lights of the trains coming toward us. We need to stay in a line."

"Meg, behind Greg. Ranger you're next. I've got the rear," Virgil said.

"I'm the one with—" Ranger clamped his mouth shut, jaw clenched at the look Virgil gave him. "Fine, Jesus. I'm the only one with a weapon though," he muttered.

"I am aware," Virgil said.

We were weaving our way through people gathered on the platform, headed for the walkway that hugged the tunnel wall just past the end of the platform. Security again, there to make sure people didn't go wandering off down the subways. He saw us approaching.

"Excuse me, you're going to need to turn around." Ooh, a polite one. Normally we get the rude ones. I mean, I'm rude, too, but generally they start it.

Greg didn't pause, he kept bearing down on the guy.

"No," he said. "Rescue mission, move."

"You're going to want to move because you don't get paid enough for this," Ranger called out from behind me.

The guy took one more half second to take in the four of us, the dark look on Greg's face, and he stepped out of our way. "Nope, I don't," he said agreeably. We filed past, headed down the walkway itself. I heard the crackle of a walkie talkie behind us. The mutter of the guy's voice, and Greg sighed.

"He just called us in, didn't he?" I asked him.

"Yes," Greg said. "Idiots are going to get themselves killed."

"Maybe they won't run across anything?" I said.

"I don't want to count on that," Greg said. We had switched on our flashlights because once we were past the platform, it didn't take long for the tunnels to get dark. The tread of our feet on the concrete echoed, and I was half leaning against the tunnel wall, listening to the Kevlar scrape against it.

What? I don't want to fall on those rails. Dying is not on my list of things to do today.

Greg paused, so we came to a stop behind him. He had his head tilted to one side. He made a frustrated noise. "I need to go ahead; I can find them faster that way."

"No," Virgil said.

"I'll come right back to—"

"No," Virgil repeated. "We don't have current maps; we don't know which section of the system he's in. The three of us cannot wait here for you to locate them and come back to us."

"We're wasting time—" Greg growled.

"Yeah, we're wasting time while the two of you argue," Ranger shot at him. "Go and come get us."

"Excuse me?" Virgil said. But Greg had already taken Ranger's advice and shot off down the tunnel ahead of us. "Don't hit any trains!" Virgil yelled after him. Then he turned on Ranger. "What the fuck are you doing?"

"He's right," Ranger said. "He can find them faster on his own, and he knows where to find us. He can come back and lead us right to them, and the sooner he finds them, the sooner we can evacuate them without Rat King being aware of it."

"We don't have to wait," I said. "He'll be able to find us; we can keep going." I started down the tunnel again.

"Whoa, no, I'm taking point in that case," Ranger said.

"No," Virgil said. "Meg can take point. Bring them out, but keep them close."

I looked back at Virgil. He stared back at me. At least, I'm pretty sure he was staring at me; between the dark and the flashlights I wasn't entirely certain. "Fine," I said. I called the whispers to me, and they came, curling against my shoulders, figures and their fingers furled against my arms and legs, the shadows rising against the tunnel walls.

"Good," Virgil said, although I could hear the strain in his voice. "Keep walking, and watch out for rats."

I started forward again, the whispers curling with me. They seemed to be having an effect on the flashlight because it was flickering. I gave it a shake, and the beam steadied for a moment then went out completely. "Damn it," I said. "Virgil, when did you put batteries in this thing?"

"They were brand new," he said. "Why are they affecting those batteries and not your phone?"

"I don't know," I said.

"Hmm. Just leave that one here for now," Virgil said. I could hear, despite the tremor, that he was planning more testing. I set the flashlight down against the wall so no one would trip over it.

The whispers were pressing on my ears, the figures sliding their fingers down my arms, the shadows stretching forward. *This way*, they said. I started forward again, one hand on the tunnel wall.

"Where are you—" I heard Ranger start, but Virgil shushed him.

"Let her operate," he said.

We continued down the walkway, but I was worried about when it would end. Did it extend the entire length? It didn't matter because before we could find out, the whispers were pulling at me, something off to our right, but we would have to go across the rails.

"Virgil, what's across from us?" I asked. Both he and Ranger lifted their flashlights up, shining them across the walls. A hole in the tunnel. Virgil hissed in a breath.

"Did he burrow?"

"They say to go that way," I said.

"Not without Greg," Virgil said.

"I don't think we can waste more time standing around waiting for him to get back," Ranger said. "We need to go look. Just tell him where we went."

Virgil swore under his breath. He had brought out his phone. "Ranger, keep your light up. I'll send him a photo, so he knows which hole in the wall I'm talking about." Virgil got the picture, texted it to Greg, and slipped his phone back in his pocket. "Let's go." Virgil took a flying leap off the walkway, landing on the other side of the tunnel, turning so his back was against the wall.

Ranger followed, and I saw Virgil's hand come up. Ranger landed at the wall, almost directly against it. "What did you do that for?!" he snapped.

"So, you didn't hit the rails," Virgil said. "Meg, come on." I backed up as far as I could, took a running leap, and felt the moment Virgil grabbed me. It was an odd sensation, less like being grabbed by a hand and more like the air around me had thickened into a pillow, engulfing but not suffocating me. He set me down much more gently next to the wall than he had Ranger.

"Seriously?" Ranger said.

"If I ran you into the wall, you wouldn't have ended up with a concussion," Virgil said. Ranger grunted.

The whispers were pulling and tugging at me again, and I stepped into the hole in the tunnel wall. Dirt walls, dirt floor, dirt ceiling. I could feel it under my fingers, and Ranger had shone the light around me to look. There was an end to it; we could see it already.

"He burrowed through the wall into the old system," Virgil said. "Greg took the long way around."

"Old system isn't blocked off?" Ranger asked.

"Of course not," Virgil said. "They need to be able to get into it to make sure it's still structurally sound and won't collapse."

I was already headed down the tunnel into the new one ahead of us. Wherever we had come out, when they built it, they were interested in form as well as function, because the walls were tiled with mosaic.

Virgil's phone pinged. He pulled it out. "He found them," he said, and I could hear the relief in his voice. "He said he's coming to us since it looks like we have a shortcut out, and he'll lead us back to them."

The steady beam of a flashlight came toward us, and then Greg had landed, a few feet from us. "Come on," he said. "We're going to need Meg so we can reach them."

"What's the situation?" Virgil asked.

"He's got them guarded by rats. I don't hear any heartbeats other than the kids and the rats, so I don't know if our assumption that he's nearby is right. There's a lot more kids than just the last few nights can account for."

Greg had already started back down the tunnel, and we were trotting to keep up. I could see the way his back tensed, and I fell back a bit. He stopped suddenly enough that Virgil and Ranger almost ran into him. The flashlight beams played off the grouping of rats in front of a doorway. They were silent and still, not even squeaking, barely breathing.

Virgil watched them for a moment. "Maybe they can't operate on independent thought anymore? To function they have to have him here telling them what to do?" His hand was on his chin. "Meg, hit them."

The whispers and I flowed forward, moving around the three men, Greg and Virgil shuddering as we passed by. The figures unfurled, shadows stretching, and when they touched the rats, they didn't even try to run, they just collapsed.

"Their hearts just stopped," Greg said.

"Hmm," Virgil said. "Good news for us."

I went through the doorway before anyone behind me could protest, although I heard the strangled noise Greg made. Ranger followed me, and the two of us stepped into the room, away from the door, so Greg and Virgil could get through. I stopped, staring.

The room was full of kids. They were crowded back against the walls, trying to get away from me. I cleared my throat and let go of the whispers. "Sorry," I said. They stayed where they were, staring back at all of us. Ranger was sweeping the flashlight across the room.

"Shit," he said. "There's, like, a hundred of them." He was right: kids of varying ages, races, sex. It would appear our Rat King wasn't picky about who he took, or where from.

"We need to chain up," Greg said, "because we don't know when he'll be back. I wasn't expecting this many; we need them all out in one go."

Virgil was already moving forward, his voice steady, reassuring, calm. "We're here to get you home. I need the youngest at the front. Everyone grab a buddy and get lined up at the door." The command in his voice floated in the air.

"There's no way they all—" but Ranger stopped whatever protest he had, because the kids were moving to obey Virgil. "How the fuck—" Ranger started a new thought.

"It's all in the tone," Virgil said. "It's the same in any language."

Fortunately, it appeared the youngest wasn't any less than six or seven. I think, I was going off height, so I could be way off. I'm not generally around kids at all.

"Okay, Meg, Ranger, I need the two of you at the front," Virgil said. "Greg and I will take the rear in case Rat King shows up while we're making our way back down the tunnels." He clapped his hands together. "Everyone hold hands!"

Almost automatically Ranger had held his hand out to

mine, looked down at it confusedly, and then snatched it back.

I snorted. There was a small hand in mine, a little girl, hair in braids, big brown eyes and umber skin, her lips trembling. "Hi," I said. "Want to get out of here?" Her fingers tightened on mine, although she gave no indication that she understood what I was saying. Maybe all the understanding she needed was that we were here to save them.

We headed out the doorway and back up the tunnel, past the tiny and sunken bodies of the rats. I could feel her hand shaking in mine, and I gave her fingers a gentle squeeze.

"What are we going to do about the rails?" Ranger asked. "We've got to get them up on the walkway, and there's too many to crowd them all in there at once." Virgil must have come to the same conclusion, because he came striding up to us past the kids.

"Ranger, I'm going to need you to stay at the door and help guard the exit while we get them across the tracks," Ranger jerked his head, and when we reached the doorway, he stopped, letting go of the little boy's hand in his, who immediately grabbed for my free hand. Virgil went through the dirt tunnel ahead of us, and the children and I followed. On the other side, before I could say anything, Virgil had snagged the little girl and the boy and I and tossed us over onto the walkway.

Well, I say tossed because I wasn't expecting it to be so sudden, and it definitely surprised the little girl because she squeaked and grabbed at me. The boy seemed unruffled. She clung to me even after we were standing on the walkway, and then Virgil was floating more kids up to me. "Meg! Take them and this," he said as he floated his flashlight over, "and start walking back. We'll catch up. Hold hands again, everyone! Single file!"

The little girl reached for the hand of the boy who was now behind her, and then we were going, walking slowly because Virgil was still tossing kids up, and I didn't want to leave anyone behind by breaking the two-by-two chain they were forming.

Plus, six-year-olds have really short legs.

I was glad I didn't have to talk because what do I say to a kid? I'm out of my depth here. Other than letting them know we're here to rescue them, I had no idea what I needed to say to be reassuring. At least I had the beam of the flashlight so we could see where we were going, but I was worried about the kids in the middle. Hopefully Virgil sends Ranger with them or something so they're not feeling their way blindly down the walkway.

Every little sound was making me tense. I was trying to keep an ear out for any squeaking, but other than our footsteps echoing off the walls, there weren't any other sounds. The kids were being incredibly quiet, and from what I knew of kids, weren't they supposed to be super loud? Maybe they understood being noisy right now would be bad.

I heard the echo of a roar. I sped up, the kids breaking into a run. I could see the lights of the station platform ahead of us; the security guy we had marched by was still there talking to uniformed officers.

"Hey! Hey!" I yelled. "Incoming!" They looked up, the officers stepping back, one of them reaching for his service weapon. "KIDS! Don't shoot!" But he had already paused, because he had seen the living chain pelting headlong behind me. The cops had backed out of my way, positioning themselves so the kids wouldn't end up falling off the walkway back on the rail, and they were crowding onto the platform, people backing up out of their way. One of the officers was speaking into the radio on his shoulder. I was surrounded by children with more pouring off the walkway, but I was trying to move back through them so I could get back down the walkway to Greg, Virgil and Ranger.

They were all clinging to my legs, and if I tried to move, I was going to trip over them. They had all flocked to me, squishing themselves as close to me and each other as they could, and now they were making noise, some crying, some excitedly chattering away, some crying and chattering at the same time. Their voices echoed in the space.

Glad some of them still viewed this as one giant adventure.

There were some very confused looking commuters staring at us. The security guy also looked confused. He looked at me and mouthed something. I shrugged. "We tried to tell you," I said, but I don't think he could hear me over the kids.

Virgil and Ranger came up the walkway behind the last of the kids. I was still trying to break free of the ones surrounding me. "Where's Greg?" I yelled. Virgil motioned back behind him.

"Making sure the giant rat back there doesn't hit a train. It saw us with the kids and took off." He was picking his way past the press of small bodies. Ranger stayed at the edge, watching the walkway.

"What about the Rat King?" I demanded. "That means he's back there, right? Why aren't we going after him?"

"Priorities," Virgil said. "Don't you dare, I know what you're thinking. We are not attempting to find him in that warren right now."

"What if he tries to take—" I started to argue, but Greg had come shooting up the tunnel, landing outside our grouping.

"What happened?" Virgil asked.

"Fucking thing just disappeared. I can't find the hole it went down. And I'm not hearing any other heartbeats down there," he was scrubbing at his face. "Did they call EMS? Child services?"

"We all just got here," I pointed out. The whispers were pressing on my ears, agitated by all the commotion, I think, and I waved them away. Too many people, too little space.

"We need to get them up to the street," Virgil said. "Come on, kids! Line up, follow me!" They scrambled to obey.

"How is he doing that?" Ranger asked, finally coming away from the walkway, and the three of us fell into step behind Virgil and the crowd of children. The cops followed us, one of them still on his radio.

I could feel eyes on my back, and I turned, but the number of commuters still on the platform was too large for me to pick out whoever had been watching us. Too much movement, too many curious eyes, a nondescript face with brown hair. Greg paused next to me. "You okay?" he asked.

"Fine," I said, turning back around. He snaked an arm around my waist while we got the kids past the turnstiles and up the stairs to the streets above.

CHAPTER THIRTEEN

Once we made it up the streets, we turned all the kids over to Detective Ross and his army of people. Virgil had called Barb and informed Ross that he had someone good with kids who was on her way, and under no conditions was he to dismiss her because she could make sure that the Rat King wouldn't be able to find the precinct or anywhere else the kids were being housed until we could take him down.

After that, we headed back to the compound. It had been one thing for Greg to find a pocket grouping of that many heartbeats, but to go searching through the subway for a single heartbeat in the dark and in an area that the Rat King had become familiar with wasn't something Virgil wanted to waste time doing. He wanted maps so we could narrow our search.

Now that we had taken back the kids he had stolen, it was likely he would move his base, so we couldn't just go back down and wait for him to come back for an ambush.

Once we were inside, Virgil turned on the news, sitting on the couch with it playing in the background while he texted and searched through something on his phone.

Ranger had taken a chair on the other side of the room. "How do you even concentrate?"

"Multi-tasking," Virgil said.

Greg and I had settled onto the couch by Virgil. Greg had an arm flung over my shoulders, one hand resting on his knee because Virgil had taken our usual spot over by the arm of the couch.

"Is there a reason we're watching the news?" I asked. Because I could think of much more entertaining shows.

Virgil grunted. "In case there's anything mysterious going on they feel like reporting that we can connect back to the Rat King that will help us locate him."

"But does it have to be this station?" I asked because Susan was the reporter up on the screen.

"No—" Virgil had started to say, but we had all gone silent because she had said Greg's hero name and mine in one and the same breath, and there was a picture of us up in the corner of the screen, in front of Barb's diner. "That—" Virgil sputtered. Because it was a picture of the moment where Greg had kissed me before we left: his hand in my hair, his lips pressed to mine, his arm around my waist, a full length shot of an interlude between us. I felt my stomach drop.

"It would appear love is in the air for those two heroes—" Susan was saying, as video came up on half the screen, below the picture of us. It was after Virgil had pulled up to the diner, Ranger stepping out, followed by Greg when he reached back for me.

We hadn't noticed the camera because there were already so many around.

They had cut the video so that it looked like the two of us had stood on the sidewalk for a bit after getting out of the car, Greg's arm around me, his nose in my hair - the moment I had tilted my head back to look up at him, when his hand came up, and he bent to kiss me.

They cut before the part where Greg had scooped me up and took off into the air, instead switching to a view of the front of the diner. Susan was still talking. "But is there dissension in the ranks of Vigilante's new team?" We watched the parking meters up and down the street suddenly bend in half in one swift motion.

Virgil was swearing. "Off the fucking record my ass." He had flung himself off the couch and was in the act of dialing when he paused to look at me. "Do you want that retracted?

Because that kiss," and he pointed a finger at the screen, "is going to be near impossible to scrub out."

Greg's arm was tense against me. "Meg," he said, and I jerked my eyes away from the screen to turn and look at him. "I don't care that they know." I could see the truth of that statement in his eyes. I had wanted our relationship to stay out of the news because I didn't think it was anyone's business, let alone Susan's, but I knew Mason and White were right. If it hadn't been her, it would've been some other intrepid reporter.

Heroes might not get the movies, the action figures, the cereals made and sold about us, but people still love to butt into our personal lives. I'll chalk it up to curiosity, but I won't let them rule how I move about the world and interact with Greg because I'm afraid of what they'll see or say about it.

"Okay," I said.

"Okay?"

"Okay," I repeated, and I snuggled into him. I could feel the tension in his arm relax. "We should ask Susan for a copy of that picture."

Greg chuckled. Kissed the top of my head. "You're planning on scaring the shit out of her at some point, aren't you?"

"Absolutely not," I said. His fingers poked me in the side.

"Liar," he said. "I know what you did to the insurance adjuster."

The news had moved on to reporting our rescue of what turned out to be 104 children of varying nationalities. At this point the FBI and INTERPOL were getting involved to help locate their families and return the children to them.

Ranger snorted. "Glad they opened that story with the important stuff."

"It is important from a certain point of view," Virgil said.

"Yeah, important to nosy people," I said.

"It's important to me," Greg said.

"I knew you were an 'only the newsworthy' type," Ranger said, leaning back into his chair, although his tone wasn't snide the way it usually was.

"Who's cooking dinner?" I asked. Virgil was still searching through his phone, having settled back on the couch now that he didn't have to go yell at studio heads.

"I am," Greg said, heaving himself up. "Come on sous chef."

Which meant Greg was just asking for my company while he cooked because I would be relegated to the side of the island that didn't have the knives and fire. But I got up anyway and followed him to the kitchen.

∞

After dinner, Greg and I ended up back in our room. Ranger and Virgil were back in the living room, watching the news for anything we could connect back to the Rat King. I sat down on the bed; Greg settled next to me and wrapped an arm over my shoulders, pulling me in close to him. He was sticking his nose in my hair again. I sighed, leaning in against him, laid my head on his shoulder and closed my eyes. I slid my hand at his back up his shirt, my right hand brushing up along his thigh, the fabric of his jeans soft, worn under my fingertips.

What? We haven't had a lot of alone time since Ranger blustered his way in. I'm going to take it when I can get it.

Because my eyes were closed, I wasn't expecting Greg's next move.

He tapped my nose, and it made me lift my head, opening my eyes to stare at him.

"Did you just boop me?" I asked.

He was grinning at me, "If you need a label for it."

There are times when his playfulness still surprises me, because he's so often serious, deliberate in his movements, even with the coiled energy that's so much a part of him.

With his strength, he has to be constantly aware of how

much force he's putting into something.

He brought his hand back up, gently pushing my hair off my face, his fingers tangled in the curls as he bent his head to kiss me.

I would say I went right for the jugular but that's in a whole different direction. My hands had moved, pulling at his pants; he huffed, laughing, and moved his arm off my shoulders to wrap it around my waist and then slid me up toward the head of the bed in one smooth motion. I grabbed at his arms, surprised, but he was still moving, his fingers brushing up my stomach, and I ended up without my shirt, on my back, his lips on my neck, his hands skimming along my ribs and stomach, his fingers teasing when he would stop just short of the undersides of my breasts.

We had knocked the pillows off the bed, and I heard threads pop when he yanked his own shirt up over his head. He worked his fingers into the band of my jeans, his mouth following in their wake, his tongue grazing along the skin, his breath tickling as he peeled my pants off. His hands were resting on my thighs as he made his way back up, slow and gentle. It made me ache, and if he didn't apply more pressure, I was going to take over and tackle him.

He could hear it, in the beat of my heart, my breath, and he chuckled, his hands sliding up until they were on my breasts, his lips on mine, and all I could think about was where his body pressed against me.

He shifted off me just enough to reach the drawer of the nightstand. I could hear it squeak because that one tends to stick, and I'm surprised Greg hasn't broken it yet.

The crinkle of a wrapper, but I wasn't listening to that, because his voice was warm in my ear, quiet but intense, a weight to his words that sent a thrill up my spine, sped up the beat of my heart.

"I love you," was all he said.

∞

The sand, the sea and the olive grove. We had started on the beach again, climbing the hill up to the grove, where we found her. Calm, cool, collected. Something brightly colored stalked through our trees, circling the two of us.

"My husband wants you," she said, one hand on a branch, pulling at the ripe fruit. We wouldn't protest; she was welcome to help herself. She had always been aloof, above us in power, handling her own offenses, but she was friendly toward us, for lack of a better word.

But it was unusual for her to be his messenger.

"Are you the second or the first?" I asked her, because hadn't there been someone else? The smell of salt in the air.

But she and her companion were gone, and we were alone among the gnarled branches, the grass pricking our feet.

∞

It was the second morning where we were woken up too early by Greg's phone ringing. With a groan, he had snagged it off the bedside table and sighed when he looked at the caller ID and answered it. "Hey, Mom. It's four in the morning. Is this important?"

He sat up, and I propped myself up. He was scrubbing at his face, pushing his hair back, and now he sounded aggravated. "Yes, that was Meg and me on the news," he sighed again. "Yes, we were unaware of the cameras. They were shooting a movie right up the street so we—" he paused. "No, the team is fine, that's just KBC trying to—" he made an irritated noise. "No, hold on, I'm going to wake Meg up if I don't—" he pulled the phone away from his face and hit the mute button. I could hear his mother on the other end, but barely. She must have been yelling at the top of her lungs for me to be able to hear her.

"I'm already awake," I pointed out to him.

"I know," he said.

"Is she yelling at you?"

"Yes."

"About?"

He leaned back and kissed me. "Doesn't matter. I'm going to go to the living room. Go back to sleep." He got up and headed out of the room.

Well, since he didn't answer me, and I wasn't getting back to sleep anyway, I dragged myself out of bed, grabbed clean clothes out of the dresser and headed for the bathroom. I almost ran into Ranger as I was coming out of our room.

"Jesus, do none of you sleep?" I said, dodging around him.

He grunted. "Virgil woke me up to ask me how my premonitions work and if I can just summon one. Where are you going?"

"The bathroom."

"No coffee?"

"Go make it yourself."

He made a frustrated noise. "I wasn't asking you to make it. Not everything out of my mouth is a challenge to how you operate."

"Good to know," I said and walked away, headed for the bathroom. Was I a little bratty with him? Hmm, maybe. But I'm not a morning person, so I don't care. If you can even call this morning.

Once I was done with a shower, I ended up outside, drinking coffee and watching the sunrise.

I'm not usually up early enough for that.

Greg, Virgil and Ranger were still inside discussing what the best tactic for going through the subways was going to be. None of them wanted to leave finding the Rat King up to chance, and Ranger can't force the premonitions, apparently. The Rat King would have to be close to making another move before he could see it happen. I had gotten bored and gone out because they kept going around in circles, arguing about whether all four of us should stick together, or if we needed to separate into teams. Greg was adamant that we should be doing a one-three since he was the only one of us who would be completely fine even if ambushed, and they were all arguing over whether the Rat King could get close enough to ambush me at all.

I got sick of it because I would go do whatever I wanted to in the subway anyway, and they all knew it.

I heard footsteps behind me, the scuff of rubber so not boots.

Greg sat down on the steps next to me with a grunt and slipped an arm around me. I leaned into him and he kissed my head. "I've got to go run by my mom's house and get our stuff. I might be a while to smooth things over."

"Your mom usually get up at 4:00 am?" I asked. It was the second night in a row that she had called him that early.

He sighed. "No, not as far as I know. She says she was up all night worrying."

"Hmm," I said. "Smooth which things over?"

"Our early exit," he said. "The not-fight with Tony."

"I don't see why you should have to smooth that over."

He paused, his arm tightening against me. "They just want what's best for me."

"You mean what they think is best for you." I knew all about people trying to push you into the decisions they want you to make - not necessarily the ones that actually work for you.

We were silent, listening to the birds singing.

"You didn't tell me your dad was a hero," I finally said. "And I thought you didn't know where he is, but Peter seems to."

Greg scrubbed at his face. "Because I don't know where he is. Peter and Tony talk to him occasionally. Supposedly they gave him my number because he asked for it, but he hasn't contacted me, and I'm not going to go look for him." There was a trace of pain in his voice, and I turned my head to look at him.

"Want me to go look for him?" I asked, the whispers brushing along the leaves at the top of the steps.

"No," Greg said.

The whispers faded, the leaves settling.

"Your mom want me to find him?"

Greg snorted, his ribs vibrating against me. "No. Don't encourage her." He moved his arm, his hand warm on the back of my neck now, fingers in my hair. "I'm going to go get our stuff. Will you be alright?"

"If Virgil goes out on a call, I'm going with him," I said. "He has to start introducing us to his clients anyway." Greg nodded and leaned in, his lips on mine. I twined my arms around his neck, pressing my body against his.

"Meg," he said, "if you keep that up, I'm—" he stopped because I moved my hands, sliding them up his shirt, his skin smooth under my fingertips. "That's not what I meant," he huffed, laughter in his voice.

"We could go up to the roof," I said, my breath in his ear, and I could feel him shiver.

"I'm going to be late," he said, but he slid a hand up my shirt, his lips on mine again. One arm tightened around me, his hand on my back; the other pulled me up against him as he started to stand.

"Ahem."

We froze and turned our heads to look at the same time.

"Timing," Greg said. I snorted, hiding my face against his neck while I giggled.

"How do you not hear him stomping around before he gets up here?" I demanded, still laughing.

Greg's voice was a whisper in my ear. "Because you're incredibly distracting."

"If you two are done," Virgil said, and I could see Ranger behind him, trying to look anywhere but at Greg and me, "I have a client call I would like Meg to accompany me on while you're running errands. If I could delay it, I would, but they're a major contributor to our operations here. Ranger has kindly agreed to go with us in case anything about the Rat King pops up in his head."

"That's not quite how that works," Ranger said.

"Do you hear it? See it? Get an overall sense of the events in your mind?"

"Yeah, but—"

"Then it pops up in your head."

Ranger scowled at him.

"We're taking the Hummer. Meg, go get suited up. You need to be dressed for this."

"Dressed for what? Scaring raccoons?"

"First impressions," Virgil said.

Greg set me down, smoothing out my shirt before he let me go. "Watch yourself," he said, giving me a kiss.

"I'll be the bane of the squirrel's existence," I quipped.

Greg chuckled, took a couple steps down, and then took off. I picked my mug up from the concrete and slid around Virgil and Ranger to go get the Kevlar.

"Meet you at the Hummer," I told them.

∞

This particular client didn't have a fence, but they did have a very long driveway with a sloping lawn leading up to their house. And on the lawn were brightly colored birds.

"Are those peacocks?" Ranger asked, leaning forward, I could feel the pressure of his hand on the back of my seat.

"Yes," Virgil said.

One of the peacocks raised his tail, the feathers spreading, vibrating. I blinked. For a moment there were eyes, and then they were gone, back to blotches of color.

The whispers were uneasy.

"Virgil," I said.

He slowed the car, looking over at me. "What is it?"

But the bird the whispers had sensed was gone.

"Nothing," I said. "Sorry, it's just the feathers…"

"They look like eyes," Ranger said. "It's kind of freaky. Not as freaky as the shit you do, but freaky."

"Hmm," Virgil said, and the car continued up the drive. He was letting it go for now, but I didn't think he was going to forget.

His client met us on her front steps. I mean, I don't know what else to call them. A portico? There were steps leading up to a space I would consider much larger than a porch, soaring columns supporting the roof above us. A mansion, in essence palatial, and between it and the moment with the peacock, I was nervous.

Displays of wealth make me anxious.

The whispers could sense it; they brushed against me, the touch of the figures' fingers on my neck. Virgil tensed. His client, a wispy, airy woman of indeterminate age, possibly because of well-applied Botox, was hanging back at the door, one hand on the knob.

"The noises are back," she said, her voice cultured with a smooth but accusing tone to it.

"Hmm," Virgil said. "Did you have someone come out and seal up the access points like I recommended?"

I could see the flicker in her eyes that meant she hadn't taken Virgil's advice.

"No," she said finally. "My husband didn't find that necessary."

"Hmm," Virgil said. "We'll take a look around. You may want to give Vengeance some extra space."

The woman shifted her eyes to me, swung the door the rest of the way open and backed away into the house. We followed her in, Virgil in the lead, Ranger at the rear armed with the baseball bat he had insisted on bringing. Virgil's shoulders were tense; the whispers were sighing in my ears. The woman, whom Virgil still hadn't introduced us to, backed further away from me.

"I'll be in the sitting room if you need me," she said, and

she walked away, heels clicking, headed somewhere into the depths of the house.

My immediate impression was *The Mysteries of Udolpho*. The interior of the house didn't seem to line up with the exterior. The inside was dark: wood paneling, dark wood floors. Glossy as they were, they felt looming, threatening. Stairs set back rose up into shadows in front of us. It was a gothic horror novel setting come to life.

What? Just because I didn't finish high school doesn't mean I don't have some greater knowledge than just pop culture. Way to be judgy. Some of us read more than just *Dracula* or *Frankenstein*. Damn.

The whispers shifted around me. Virgil took another step away from me. "Vengeance?" he asked.

"Sorry," I said, but the whispers didn't want to go. "They're…" They were agitated. Something was in the house, but they couldn't tell me what.

Virgil was watching me. "Where do they want to go?"

"Anywhere but here," I said. It was the closest I could tell him to what they were trying to tell me. Because the impression was more than when they would echo me, or the one-word warnings when something immediate was about to happen. They did not want to go any deeper into the house.

Virgil was considering my answer, his brow furrowed. "If I could humor them right now I would. First or second floor?"

I was trying to listen, but the whispers were rushing around me. "I can't get a clear answer," I finally admitted.

"Okay, I'm sending you to the second floor. Ranger, stick close to her. I've got the first floor and basement." He looked Ranger square in the face. "I recommend you take my advice under consideration."

Ranger gave him a jerk of his head, held out a hand to indicate the stairs. "Ladies first," he said.

"Why do I feel like that's a ploy so I get picked off by the monsters and you get time to run?" I grumbled but headed up the stairs. Ranger kept pace with me as we climbed.

"I thought that was supposed to be chivalrous, having ladies go first."

"I don't think it is; I think it's more, here, you go in first in case there's danger ahead. Then when you die, I have time to get away."

He chuckled.

The whispers and figures flowed around us; I could hear their fingers sliding across the wood. At the top of the stairs, the hallway was dark, too, cloaked in shadows, more dark wood paneling. The dark wood of the floor was covered with dark runners. The darkness of my shadows was the only thing that stood out against it in this place. The hallway was lined with doors.

We both paused. "If all of Virgil's clients have houses like this, no wonder they're constantly calling about squirrels in the attic. I'd be paranoid about every little noise too," Ranger said.

I stayed silent, not wanting to admit that I was just as creeped out as the whispers seemed to be.

"Well, we need to pick a direction," Ranger said. "Left or right?"

"Flip a coin?" I asked. Because the only direction I wanted to go was back down the stairs and out the door.

To our left, we heard a muffled thud.

Ranger brought the bat up. "Get behind me."

"Oh, now you want to be in front," I said, but I let him draw ahead of me, the whispers, figures, shadows, and I following in his wake.

Ahead of us, one of the doors was agape. "Door number one?" Ranger asked.

"You're the one leading this parade, so you get to go first."

He turned to smirk at me. "Scared?"

Ahead of us, the hinges creaked as the door swung further open. He took a hurried step back, twisting to face the door, raising his free arm to block me.

Now I was smirking, stepping around his arm to crouch, one hand extended. "You don't belong here."

The raccoon stood on its hind legs, one paw on the frame of the door, staring at us. It hissed at me.

"Rude," I told it. The whispers giggled in my ears.

The raccoon, who apparently gave no fucks, dropped to all four feet and waddled off down the hall away from us.

"So," said Ranger, "are we supposed to catch it?"

"Be my guest," I said. "Watch out for its teeth."

Ranger snorted. "I know how to handle raccoons. Go get Vigilante, we don't want to touch it with our bare hands."

I hesitated. The whispers were pulling at me. "Why don't we?"

"You think they're called trash pandas for no reason? They're disease carriers. Don't touch it. Have Vigilante float it out a window or something."

I definitely didn't want to go downstairs by myself. Instead, I pulled out my phone and sent Virgil a text. Ranger watched me.

"Seriously?" he said.

"It's faster than me going downstairs to look around for him. Get him up here with you and then relocate the raccoon," I said. Plus, everyone knows what happens to the first person to wander off from the group. Oh, shit, we've already split up. Meh, I'm sure Virgil is fine.

"Where's it going to go?"

I pointed. "It's already going." And it had; it had reached the end of the hallway and turned a corner, disappearing from view.

"Wait or follow?" Ranger asked.

I didn't answer because we could hear footsteps coming up the stairs. Virgil can move quickly when he wants to. He emerged from the shadows. "Where is it?"

"It went down the hall," Ranger said.

Virgil sighed and strode off down the hallway and

around the corner.

"Should we be following him?" Ranger asked.

"I'm sorry, am I supposed to be holding your hand for this entire operation?" I headed down the hallway, leaving Ranger to wait or catch up. He chose to catch up.

"Look, I know I did something to piss you off. I'm trying to make it right. I'll back off, missions, personal life, whatever. You take the lead." He put a hand on my arm, and we stopped, barely to the corner of the hall. "Just, if I ever have a chance, let me know. Until then, whatever space you need."

I took a step back, and he let his hand drop. "You will literally never have a chance."

"I feel like I will though," he said, grinning at me. The whispers giggled, misting out at my shoulders. "No, not the freaky shit. Not needed!" He was backing down the hallway, pointing at me. "Friends?"

"I'll take your application into consideration."

We caught up in time to watch Virgil perform a hands-free toss of the raccoon out a window.

"I hate those things," he told us.

CHAPTER FOURTEEN

Greg still wasn't back when we reached the compound. As soon as he had the Hummer parked in the garage, Virgil pulled out his phone. Ranger and I followed him up the stairs. Whoever he was calling didn't answer, so he called again. And then again. He swore when it went to voicemail for the third time. "Meg, call Greg, he's not answering my calls."

I pulled out my phone. It rang once, and then Greg's voice was on the other end. "Are you alright?" he asked, anger laced with concern.

"I'm fine. Why aren't you answering Virgil?"

"I have to go—"

"What? What do you—"

"Not you," he said. "Hold on." His voice was distant; he must have pulled the phone away from his face. "No, mom, I've got to go. Yeah, love you, too. Thanks for lunch." Then he was back. "You still there?"

"What's going on? Why weren't you answering?"

A sigh. "Can I explain when I get back?"

"Okay," I said. I wanted an explanation now.

He must have heard it in my voice, his tone softening. "Love you, I'll be home soon. Have Virgil keep the garage open; I'll be coming in hot."

He hung up before I could answer him. I looked at Virgil. "He said he'll explain when he gets here. Oh, and open the garage."

Virgil snorted and stalked back down to the garage. "He better not wreck my cars."

194

I went back to my room and closed the door so I could change. I tossed the hero outfit aside, back in just jeans and a tee, took my hair down and shook it out. I headed out to go to the living room, but Ranger was still in the hallway, that blank, distant look on his face. He snapped to, looked around, and focused on me.

"Call him back."

"Why? What's going to happen?" But Ranger was already grabbing my arm and pulling me toward Virgil's room for the garage entrance.

"Rat King, in the city again. We need to catch him."

I yanked my arm away. "Wait!" I rushed into my room and grabbed the stupid outfit.

Look, I promised Greg I would try to remember it. If I hadn't just changed, I probably would've forgotten it. But the Kevlar might be needed. Back out in the hallway, we were headed down the stairs.

"Rat King!" Ranger was calling out.

Virgil swore. "Hummer, damn it." He swung himself up in it, Ranger and I seconds behind him.

I was trying to struggle into the outfit and call Greg back at the same time, but it was going to voicemail. Ranger was in the passenger seat, trying to talk Virgil through what he was seeing.

"Big, empty room, walkways—" he was saying.

"Warehouse. Which warehouse?"

"I don't – try staying on the road!"

"I am on the road," Virgil said calmly. "Which warehouse?"

Ranger was silent, head cocked to the side. He straightened up. "The docks, a warehouse at the docks."

"He's trying to run," Virgil said. "It's now or never."

My phone rang, I fumbled it. "Hey!"

"Thought you were going to leave the garage open for me. I almost crashed," Greg sounded like he wasn't sure if he should be irritated.

"Rat King," I said. "Hold please." I hit speaker, grabbed Ranger's hand and slapped the phone into it. "Hold that, keep talking, he'll be able to hear you."

"Which warehouse? Can you see a number? Lettering?" Virgil was still quizzing him.

"B— B something. God damn it, it's not normally this vague!"

"It's Meg," Virgil said, still calm. "Something about her is messing with your accuracy. Just keep trying."

"Every event with Meg there comes in vague. Even the bank was vague and I hadn't met her yet," Ranger snapped. "Why?"

"If you could summon one to start with, we could try testing this," Virgil said. "As it is, focus on this vision please."

"Maybe you should be taking notes," I said, "so we don't have to do separate testing, ever."

"Who says I'm not? Now, focus."

The Hummer was roaring up the road, flashing past mailboxes, and then Virgil took a left. I would say the tires squealed, but the weight of the Hummer wouldn't quite let them make that sound. It was more like a deep thrumming. Then we were speeding down the highway, dodging traffic. Virgil was moving cars out of the way.

"Greg doesn't like it when you do that," I said.

"Greg's not here. What he doesn't know won't hurt him."

"Speaker phone," said Greg.

"Then what did I just do that you don't like?"

Ranger was motioning at us. "Would you stop? I can't hear it!" he paused, then, "B23! Fuck. It shouldn't be this difficult."

"Did you hear that? Warehouse B23 down at the docks. Keep the giant rat off the rest of us while we look for the Rat King," Virgil announced.

"Got it. Meet you there," Greg said and hung up. Ranger handed the phone back to me.

My outfit wasn't positioned correctly, sitting too low at the chest. I gave up on it. It was good enough. I slipped the phone into one of the pockets, climbed into a seat and buckled in.

"Meg, have you not been belted in this whole time?" Virgil said, turning to look at me, while Ranger yelled "Road!" at him.

"What Greg doesn't know won't hurt him," I said.

∞

The docks were gated and locked. Virgil stopped the car and studied them for a minute. "How much time do we have?" he asked.

"Not much," Ranger said.

Virgil raised a hand, and with a shriek, the gate flung itself out of the way. Then he gassed the car, and we roared down the roadway, flying past the buildings to our left, the docks, ships and water to our right. Where was everyone? Would we be finding bodies once we had taken the Rat King down?

Ranger pointed, "There, there!" Virgil hit the brakes, and the Hummer came to a quick and sudden stop, throwing me forward into the belt.

"Ow," I said.

"That's why you always wear your seatbelt." Virgil was climbing out of the driver's side; Ranger was grabbing the baseball bat he had set on the floor. He was around and pulling open my door before I could.

"You coming?" he asked me, giving the bat a spin. I hopped out.

"How much longer do we have?" Virgil said. "We should wait for Greg if we can."

Ranger tilted his head again. "If we wait, he's going to leave the warehouse, and then we're going to have to chase him down. I can see the alleys."

"Okay, we're going in. Meg, at the rear."

I flared up. "I should be going in first to clear things back." Virgil paused, so I pressed my argument. "What's he going to do? He's using rats, and as long as I stay clear of the big one and its tail, I'll be fine."

"Okay, full range. Ranger, stay with her in case she needs physical defense. Once we're in and have the lay of the land, we can break off and go searching." Virgil backed away from me. "Go, Meg."

Ranger stepped up next to me, and I called to the whispers. They came, curling around my shoulders, the figures furling down my arms, up my legs, before they flowed outward, sighing as they went, circling us as they reached the edge. We stepped up to the door, the figures billowing back toward me, and Ranger kicked it in. I slipped past him, the figures and shadows reaching forward before rising and circling back again.

The warehouse was full of zombie rats. There were so many they were having to climb over each other, squeaking and scurrying, scratching and clawing as they tried to flee from me. The figures rushed them, the whispers howling, and the rats burst. Ranger and I moved forward, stepping slowly, because in a moment we were going to have to walk through the remains to reach more. I pulled the figures toward me.

"What are you doing?" Ranger asked, the bat raised and ready.

"Giving Virgil room to get in. He can't get past me otherwise."

Ranger nodded, stepping around to put his back against mine.

I could hear shrieking squeals as Virgil came in and started throwing rats out of his way and into range of the figures. I heard them squeal again as they burst. I looked back over my shoulder. He was making his way over to a set of stairs on the other side of the room.

"Where's the big one?" Ranger was asking. "There's always been a big one, too."

"I don't know."

A distant roar. Then another, and another.

"Oh, fuck," Ranger said.

"You jinxed us." I sent the figures back out; the rats that had been pressing forward got caught by the figures as they swirled outward. Desperate squeals echoed as they fell back, scrambling out of range.

I felt the impact when Greg landed, the ground shaking under my feet.

"Does he do that for the dramatic effect?" Ranger asked.

I didn't answer because in that moment Greg had come inside and started crushing the rats that were in his way. They were trying to swarm him and drag him down, so he shot straight up among the walkways and rafters, and they fell. The ones that managed to hold onto him he grabbed and flung at the walls.

Rangers and I were moving forward again, headed for a space that looked like an office under the walkways, the figures swaying through the air. Ranger was out in front, taking out the rats that the figures and shadows couldn't reach as they scurried away.

Another roar: pounding, scraping and the cracking of wood in the wall furthest from us. Part of the wall exploded outward, a gaping hole in the wood.

This time there were three of them.

Greg dove at the first one that came through. He tackled it, and it stumbled backwards, knocking into the two trying to come through the wall behind it. I felt the ground shake again.

Ahead of me I saw Ranger hesitate as he turned to face me. "We need to find the Rat King before one of these things gets out. You got the zombies?"

"Yes."

He gave me a jerk of his head and then leapt out past the range of the figures; a gust of air, and the zombie rats trying to reach him slowed. He took them out as he ran past, headed for another door in the wall.

He had given me an idea. But I was going to have to get bloody. Gross.

I pulled the figures and shadows to me, the rats surging forward, and then I ran and leapt at them, the figures swirling out to slam into the rats, who burst. I landed in the middle, skidded in a puddle of blood but caught myself, the shadows hitting the floor with me and spilling out, black ink mixed with the red. The figures took out any of the rats who stayed in their range with me.

The rats who had managed to scramble away stared at me. The quivering mass of more bodies beyond them. I stared back. And then I ran forward and leapt at them again.

It became the nastiest game of tag I've ever played.

I chased the rats around the warehouse, the figures eddying around me, pulling in and flowing out, shadows rising and crashing. The whispers were laughing in my ears. A couple of times I fell, landing hard on my hands and knees, slipping and sliding in blood and entrails.

From the roaring, screaming and crashing next door, it seemed Virgil had joined in on Greg's fight.

But there was no more movement around me. As far as I could tell, all the rats in the room with me were dead, and I was covered in gore. I tried rubbing it off my hands onto my pants, but that didn't help since they were already bloody. In fact, I think it made it worse.

The whispers and figures curled back against my shoulders, furling along my arms, shadows stretching from my feet. "We good to go?" I asked them. Assent from the whispers. They could sense him. The figures brushed my hands with theirs, their fingers sliding along my skin.

The only place I knew that hadn't been checked was the little office ahead of me, so we were going to start there.

Stepping around and over the zombie rats, I headed for it. The door slammed open, the figures swirled outward, but he was too far from me for them to reach.

"Don't move," he snarled at me. There was a pistol pointed at my chest.

And I recognized him. He was the guy I thought was a cop at the charity event.

Guess I should've killed him. Sucks for me.

I'll never be sure which order things happened in, or if they were simultaneous. The flash of the muzzle, the crack of a gunshot, and the sensation of being punched in the chest, high on the sternum, right where I had left the Kevlar too low. It was odd, how at that moment, my only concern was that Greg was going to be upset with me.

I crumpled.

But now the shadows had a target. I could feel their rage. It makes them stronger. I heard screaming, the snapping of bone, wet ripping and tearing.

And then the whispers were back, pulling at me, but my breath was coming in ragged gasps, and I couldn't stay. I felt it, the moment when my heart stopped.

Someone was screaming my name.

I was falling, and the whispers fell with me. We spiraled down into darkness and silence.

It engulfed us.

∞

When I came to, I was standing on sand. The whispers and figures were curling against my back, pressed to my skin, their fingers brushing my hair and face, shadows pooled at my feet. This, that I was still here, connected to them, was unexpected.

At first it seemed like there was nothing there but them, the sand and me.

But then there was a wind, scuffing across the grains, tumbling it over itself, blowing grit into the air. The figures and I watched it, and with the wind came sound. Someone called for me, a howl of pain and anguish that made me ache down to the bone.

Did I have bones here? Wherever here was. I knew I existed, but it felt formless, vague, shadowed.

I needed to go back. The whispers agreed. As one, we turned, looking for a way back out.

The walls formed at that point. Or had they already been there? Stone cliffs, rising above us, a circle. My gaze traveled upwards; the top of them was so far away, and across the mouth of this well was a lightning storm. Brilliant flashes of light crawled from cloud to cloud.

Great, I'm in a giant, cylindrical stone prison, and the only way out is to go up. I started toward the walls.

Time stretched, and I stopped because the walls weren't getting any closer, which made me turn and look around. There were my footprints, the wind wiping them away. I saw them long enough to see I had just walked in a circle, which didn't seem possible.

The whispers sighed in my ears; we couldn't get out that way.

"Well then how?" I asked them, irritated. My voice echoed so loudly in the space that I winced.

Shhh, the whispers said. *Don't wake them.*

There was a rustling, an almost drumroll-like rattle to my left. I turned to look.

It was a peacock, its tail feathers spread, and in the feathers were eyes. The eyes blinked at me. I staggered back from it. I knew whom it belonged to.

Guardian, the whispers told me. I wanted to snap at them that I knew that but didn't want to attract any more attention, so I bit my tongue.

The peacock turned and walked away from me.

With it, there was another voice in the wind. This one was commanding; an edge of – malice? – was the closest I could think to compare it to, but it was more than that. It was malevolence and rolling thunder.

"Megaera," it said. Its deep timbre echoed around me.

I did not want this thing's attention; I could feel it in my bones, resonating through me, or what there was of me. Attracting his attention didn't end well for a lot of people.

I had the vague sense of a hand in the air, someone tall, with thick, dark, curling hair, the gleam of a bronzed body. The tales always painted him as attractive. They glorified beauty, often above all else, ignoring the villain that he was.

"Join me, little one," he said.

The whispers and I tried to back away, but I was against the stone walls. I didn't know how or when I had reached them. The stone was cold on the tips of my fingers. The whispers hissed, figures swaying, circling, shadows rising. They spoke to him. *We follow no one*, they said, sibilant and fierce, their many voices echoing, and with theirs, I could hear my own, although my lips were still.

The hand withdrew; the whispers and I waited on edge. Would he react with anger? I knew he could crush me. I could feel the power in him, even in this prison, and he had always been easily offended.

An amused chuckle. "You follow no one," he agreed, and then the voice darkened. "For now." And the whispers knew: *they* had found their anchors.

Then it was just the sand, the whispers, the figures, the shadows and me.

∞

It felt like there was a hand in my chest, squeezing my heart, and I tried to hit at it, but there wasn't anything there to hit. I wasn't even sure I managed to lift my hand in the first place. I could feel the cold of the concrete seeping up into my back, the slick of blood beneath my fingers.

I took a breath. One long gasp, and then I was coughing. My lungs were burning, like they had been filled with more than just air.

Virgil's voice sounded above me. "Get her on her side."

Someone rolled me, and now I was lying on my left, Virgil's hands on my face, "Meg. Meg, open your eyes, I want to check your pupils." He sounded worried. I had never heard him sound anything but cool in a crisis.

I tried to sit up, but someone was holding me down, pressing down on my right side. "Let go," I rasped. I was yanking my arm away from them, trying to get both arms under me so I could push myself up. The whispers swirled around me. The hands were gone.

Virgil had jerked away. "God damn it, Meg, stop!"

I couldn't stop. There was something I had to tell them, something important, but it was fading. The whispers settled, sliding across my skin.

"Meg," Ranger's voice was snapping at me. "Let us help you." His hand was on my arm.

"Greg and I can't get past them; they need to go."

The whispers were agitated, trying to help me remember, and I needed to tell them before the whispers would leave. The message finally worked its way across my brain. "They're coming," I told them. The whispers retreated, and I was surrounded by hands.

∞

When I woke up, the tableau was strangely familiar. Virgil's lab, hospital bed, Greg across the room in a chair, head in hands. The way he looked up when I opened my eyes, the way he staggered as he rushed to me. But this time he pulled me up into his arms, his face against mine, and kissed me.

At least I got to wake up in one piece this time instead of patchworked back together.

Greg's shoulders were shaking, a tremor in his arms. I wrapped my arms around him, hands resting on his back, ignoring the way the IV attached to me pulled at my skin, and we sat there on the bed, huddled against each other.

"What happened?" I asked.

"You got shot," Greg said, his voice thick. He pulled back to look at me.

"I vaguely remember that part, yes," I said. It hadn't hurt quite as much as I was expecting. "But what happened after that?"

"The uh," and he seemed to be having trouble speaking, his eyes on mine, like he was worried I would suddenly fade away, "the uh, giant rats just collapsed. We found you—" he paused again, shuddered. "You were on the floor, and I couldn't hear your heart—" he stopped, and with a sob he pulled me back into his chest, nose in my hair. His body trembled against mine. I squirmed so I could raise my face to his. There were tears running down his cheeks.

"Do you need my shirt?" I asked him.

It surprised a laugh out of him. He was wiping at his face, and I raised my hands, swiping tears away with my thumbs.

"I don't think Virgil left you your shirt," he said. "It wasn't salvageable."

"My bill for attire has skyrocketed ever since I started hanging out with you guys."

He laughed again and kissed me, one hand in my hair, one on my back.

The lab door opened, and Greg raised his face away from mine.

"I know, timing," Virgil said. He came over to the bed and held out a mug. "I come bearing gifts."

I took the coffee. "I see a gift."

"Semantics," Virgil said.

"What happened?" I asked.

"You died," Virgil said.

"Looks like I got better," I said. Greg made a strangled noise. "What?" I said. "Obviously I'm not still dead. Ergo, I got better."

"References aside," Virgil said, "Ranger reversed the damage. I had to restart your heart, and overall, it was a close call. Death has much shorter time limits than broken arms apparently. I think we were all shocked it worked at all."

"Don't get shot again, got it," I said.

Greg made another strangled noise, his arms tightening around me. "Coffee," I told him, and he loosened his grip.

"I think you're being too blasé about this for Gregor's peace of mind," Virgil said. Greg shot him a glare. Virgil ignored it. "You gave us a message when we got you back."

"I did?"

"Yes, you did. You said, 'They're coming.' Who's they?"

I had to take a minute to think. But all that came up was a blank wall, the impression of sand and wind and nothing more. No other information. "I can't remember."

Virgil uncrossed his arms, one hand up at his chin - the thinking pose. "Would the whispers know?"

Next to me Greg tensed. I could feel the tremor still in his hands. "Can I wait to ask them?"

Virgil nodded. "I think I can give you a few minutes of privacy."

I was thinking more like a couple days, but when Virgil has a grip on a thought, he's not going to let it go. I sighed. "Did any of your contacts ever get back to you about the Rat King?"

I was hoping the subject change would distract Virgil for a few hours at least, and from the look he gave me, he knew and wasn't going to fall for it.

"Yes," he said.

"And?" I prompted when he didn't seem inclined to say anything else. "How was he getting the kids without anyone seeing anything?"

"As far as they can tell from what they've found, the rats were chewing through wires on any cameras that would let them trace their path. I'm having them look into any thefts of items that translate into quick cash, things missing from private collections, even thefts of food, but that will take time to track down. As for the children, since none of them were over the age of ten, we're assuming he had the ability to control them the same way he was controlling the rats. Since he's dead, we can't ask him," he paused, his hand up at his chin. I don't know how he manages to look like he's studying me over the rims of glasses when he doesn't wear any, but he does. "I'll be back once you've had a chance to rest."

"Okay."

Virgil nodded, went out the door, and closed it behind him. I heard the lock click into place.

The gesture was appreciated.

"How do you feel?" Greg asked me.

"I feel fine, for having, you know, died."

I saw the shadow flit across his face. He cupped my face with one hand. "Don't do it again."

"Yeah, I'm completely closed to a repeat experience of that." What? Just because I don't remember what happened doesn't mean I should be chancing getting brought back to life again. Bet you that you only get one.

He smiled at me, but it was sad. "Can I convince you to retire?"

"Nope, sorry. I kind of like this whole saving the world business."

He pulled me against him, plucked the mug from my hand and set it on the bedside table. "I'm going to talk to Virgil about a better way to keep you outfitted."

I snuggled into him. "You do that. I promise to wear it." And I meant it.

He sighed. "I love you, too."

∞

When Virgil had finally come back, Greg would only retreat as far as the door. I had tried to insist I felt fine and could get up, but since I had apparently been out of it for a couple days after I got brought back to life, Virgil felt it would be prudent for me to stay in the lab, at least until we were sure everything was in working order, including my ability to call the whispers.

I had made them let me get out of the damn hospital bed, though. Stupid paper gown or not. If I'm not recovering from being seriously injured, I don't give a shit what anyone sees.

Virgil stayed by the door with Greg. "Ready, Meg?"

"Yup," I said, and I called to them. They came, slithering up my legs, fingers curling over my shoulders, shadows pooling at my feet, the whispers sighing in my ears. I could hear and feel relief in their touch. I was theirs and they were mine.

"Can they tell us who they are?"

I asked as they swirled around me: who is coming? *The others*, they told me. But the others who? *The others; they have their anchors now. They are theirs and they were theirs.* And they could feel my frustration at the riddle, and so they were agitated, rushing around me.

"What are they saying?" Virgil asked me.

"Something about the others, but they can't tell me what that means." And the whispers repeated, *they have their anchors.* "Anchors, they have their anchors." I echoed them. Their ability to communicate with me had become stronger, apparently. This was way more than one-word answers, fleeting impressions and emotions.

"Like you?" Virgil said.

"What do you mean, like me?" I asked, startled.

"Do they mean an anchor like you're their anchor?"

I'm pretty sure I stared at Virgil long enough for him to wonder if I had gotten brain damage from dying. I had forgotten we had told him that, the whispers and I. But the whispers were laughing in my ears. *Yes, like you. You are ours.* I got the feeling that the figures liked Virgil.

"They say yes," I told him.

"That sounds like it's bad." Greg said.

Virgil grunted. "It certainly doesn't sound good. Not if Meg's power is warning us about them in the first place." He stood there, hand on chin, for another moment. "Okay, Meg, get some rest, we might need to expand the team, and if we're doing that we're going to need to move. This space is getting too small." He went out the door.

The whispers and figures were still circling me, fingers brushing my face. Greg was waiting patiently, leaning against the doorframe. I let them go, and they gave a knowing giggle as they faded.

Then I remembered. Greg had said he would explain why he wasn't answering his phone when he got back. But that got interrupted by the Rat King.

But first, clothes. Because if we got into an argument, I didn't want to be at the disadvantage of being mostly unclothed. I headed for the door.

"Move," I said, because he was in my way. He just crossed his arms.

"Where are you going?" he asked me.

"I want clothes. I feel fine; I think I can make it as far as our room." He watched me for a beat, and then stood aside. I slipped past him, and he followed me down to our room, and he closed the door behind us before he leaned back against it. I tossed the hospital gown on the floor and started pulling clothes out. I could feel his eyes on me.

I might have done a little more wiggling than was absolutely necessary to get dressed.

"You're incorrigible," he said.

"Hmm," I said. "So, why weren't you answering your phone?"

The subject change must have surprised him because he answered immediately instead of giving the long considering pause he usually did when I put him on the spot. "I was arguing with my mom."

"About?"

"You," he said, surprising me, because usually it was like

pulling teeth to get answers out of him.

"What about me?"

He scrubbed at his face. "What kind of future I could possibly have with another hero. You would think after my dad…" He sighed. "Doesn't matter. I told her it wasn't any of her business whether I had a future with another hero. She said she just wants me to be happy."

I felt like I had unknowingly stepped up to a cliff. The question was there, at the tip of my tongue, but did I want to know? What kind of future was he looking for, and was I ready for it?

Look, I died. There's nothing more introspective than coming back from death, but that doesn't mean I can deal with making plans. I'm more a fly by the seat of my pants kind of girl. I don't know that I'll ever be ready for the path Greg wants to take. If he wants that path, he's going to have to spring it on me. I hear Vegas is nice. Do they do fly through chapels?

Oh, shit, am I seriously considering marriage?

My thoughts chased themselves in circles while he stood against the door watching me. Which question did I want to ask him?

I could just let it lie.

What? I can absolutely let things go. Shut up.

He was still waiting.

"Lock the door," I said.

He chuckled, but he locked the door. He strode over to me, hands hovering. "Are you sure you're okay?"

"Fit as a fiddle," I said, and I kissed him.

What? You thought I was going to ask what's in his sock drawer? You know me better than that by now.

∞

Virgil had officially asked Ranger to join us. Although it had appeared that he had little to no choice in the matter, because as far as Virgil seemed to be concerned, Ranger was staying regardless of invitation status.

Ranger said he would on one condition: that Virgil relocate downtown. Otherwise, Ranger was finding a place in the city anyway. He said he needed his own space, wanted to be closer to where the action was happening, because having to tear off for hour long drives wasn't working for him, and oh, he needed some fucking windows.

Since Virgil had already decided on moving anyway, he was more than amenable to Ranger's demands. It was just a case of finding the right building and getting the funding. It's not like he can just sell the compound to someone else. And he wasn't going to sell it anyway; it makes a good safe house.

Also, where else was he going to park the helicopter?

Yeah, I know, he won't use it, he prefers to drive. He just likes being able to tell people he has one.

Plus, Susan had his address. So, he wanted to make it hard for her to find us again. She hasn't told him how she got it, but he has his suspicions.

Apparently our aborted interview and lack of any other information meant she felt free to not only ignore the off the record rule but to give out his phone number.

The four of us were having breakfast, arguing, I mean discussing, what kind of amenities and defenses our new location was going to need when Virgil's phone rang. He looked at it for a moment and then answered. "Who is this?"

His eyes narrowed. "How did you get this number?" A pause while he listened. "Oh, did she now?" Another listening pause. "No, I don't think she will, but I'll pass on the message." I could feel Greg tense on the stool next to me. Ranger straightened up; he must have heard the venom in Virgil's voice.

"What?" I asked. Virgil waved a hand at me. "Don't shush me, what?"

"Hanging up now," Virgil said. He set the phone down. It was silent for a moment, and then rang again. Virgil hit ignore call and looked at me. "Don't break my stuff."

"What?" I asked again. I was starting to feel like a broken record.

"That was your parents. They said they want to see you."

I could feel the whispers calling to me, but Greg's hand was warm on my back, and I focused on that. The whispers sighed and faded; they would be here when I needed them. I raised my chin. "Tell them I said no."

We went back to our discussion. If they called him again at any point that day Virgil didn't tell me.

ABOUT THE AUTHOR

Jamie lives in Charlotte, NC with her husband, three feral children and two badly behaved dogs.

She has BAs in English and Theatre, her favorite part of which was working backstage on traveling Broadway productions.

www.ingramcontent.com/pod-product-compliance
Lightning Source LLC
Chambersburg PA
CBHW020946180626
46814CB00003B/954